Washington City
is Burning

Books by Harriette Gillem Robinet

Ride the Red Cycle

Children of the Fire

Mississippi Chariot

If You Please, President Lincoln

Washington City Is Burning

Washington City
is Burning

Harriette Gillem Robinet

A JEAN KARL BOOK

ATHENEUM BOOKS FOR YOUNG READERS

Atheneum Books for Young Readers
An imprint of Simon & Schuster Children's Publishing Division
1230 Avenue of the Americas
New York, New York 10020
The text of this book is set in Monotype Bulmer.
First Edition
Printed in the United States of America
10 9 8 7 6 5 4 3 2 1
Library of Congress Cataloging-in-Publication Data
Robinet, Harriette.
Washington City is burning / Harriette Gillem Robinet. — 1st ed.
p.   cm.
"A Jean Karl book."
Summary: In 1814 Virginia, a slave in President Madison's White House,
experiences the burning of Washington by the invading British army.
ISBN 0-689-80773-2
1. United States—History—War of 1812—Juvenile Fiction. [1. United States—History—
War of 1812—Fiction. 2. Washington (D.C.)—History—Capture by the British, 1814—
Fiction.] I. Title.
PZ7.R553Was   1996
[Fic]—dc20
95-33382

SCALE OF POLES

GEORGE TOWN

Rock Creek

College

Masons I.

PRESIDENTS
HOUSE

TIBER

P O T O M A C   R I V E R

BRIDGE

REFERENCES

			Square No.
Presbyterian Church	Do	F	225
Do	Do	South Cap	656
Episcopal	Do	16	200
Do	Do		877
Friends	Do	1	106
Baptist	Do	1&19	118
Do	Do		822
Methodist	Do	G&14	252
Do	Do		822
Catholic	Do	F	570
Do	Do	South Cap	654
Marine Barracks			927
General Post Office / Patent Office		E	151
Infirmary			448
Orphan Asylum		7	128
Masonic Hall		B	525
Theatre		C	540

VIRGINIA

West Front of the Capitol

A

CORRECT MAP

of the

CITY of WASHINGTON

(Capital)

of the

UNITED STATES OF AMERICA

Lat. 38.53 N? Long. O. C.

Eng? by W.I. Stone Wash?

1820

CAPITOL

EASTERN BRANCH

North Front of the President's House

Chapter One

Herein I, Virginia of Madison, will tell the true story of the August of my twelfth year. I entered that month like a staggering caterpillar, and emerged a winged butterfly. Although I am a slave, my writing will be that of an educated child, having since that August been well taught in rhetoric, grammar, and composition. And please, dear reader, judge me gently.

On Monday, August 1, 1814, I rode beside Tobias on the Madison chariot-and-four. No ordinary carriage, the Madison chariot was reddish brown outside, decorated with yellow lace inside, and built specially for the president of these United States.

This was the first time I had ever ridden on the chariot, and I sat, a slave child, nonetheless pleased as a princess.

It had been an exciting six-day journey from the Madison estate of Montpelier in Orange, Virginia. A hot six-day journey. At the inn in Alexandria a man had told us the mercury was near a hundred, but our master's young horses had enjoyed the run. Road dust shimmered at our feet like gold, and blue-green dragonflies hung in the hot air.

Along sunny stretches of the rolling hills of Virginia Tobias had taught me to drive the chariot. Although he thought I should take driving seriously, I felt driving was a lark. Like eagles those horses flew for me, until Tobias slowed them down.

"Tobias," I now asked with a toss of my braids, "how is it I was chosen by Miss Dolley to be of service at the President's House?"

Ahead of us a summer green maple lent shade to the golden dust of the road we traveled. Tobias did not answer, but slowed our four pretty bay horses, and we stopped in the kindness of that shade. The hum of insects was like music to my ears. When he had unhitched the horses to allow their drinking at a roadside horse trough, he turned to me.

I saw worry in the lines of his wrinkled brown face.

"Virginia," he began, as he stood below me on the

road, "you done proved yourself a child loyal to our people of African ancestry."

He was speaking about my bravery of January past. I shrugged. "Surely the mistress knows nothing. . . ."

Suddenly I was suspicious. I stared at him. "Tobias," I whispered, "it is you who want me in Washington, and not our mistress. Does she know nothing of my coming?"

In seconds my feelings changed from delight to dread. The master expected me to be working in his mansion at Montpelier. Was I now a runaway slave? Why had Tobias gotten me into trouble?

As I stood in the driver's seat, I felt the stiffness and ache in the back of my legs. This tightness of the burn scars was enough of suffering. With fright in his eyes, Tobias climbed nimbly to the driver's footboard. At twelve years I stood taller than he, but only because he himself was a hunchback.

"Virginia," he whispered, "there be much for you to be doing. Miss Dolley be a kindly mistress; she be pleased to see you. On my word." He took a deep breath.

I plopped down on the hard wooden seat and stomped my feet. Before my night of bravery, they had said I was a silly girl, dillydallying in my work. After that one night, other slaves thought me brave.

Sitting beside me now, Tobias shook my elbow.

"Virginia, you be a child to enjoy the parties, the cool pineapple, the ice cream, the picnics by Rock Creek."

I wiped tears from my eyes, untied the ribbon beneath my chin—the ribbon from my frilly yellow cap. Tobias had insisted I wear yellow today. Today! The day we would reach Washington City. Yellow was Miss Dolley Madison's favorite color. I always suspected my beloved Tobias was a crafty man.

"Tell me," I asked, "just what is it you want me for?"

"Not all be trustworthy, not all be loyal to our people."

"I am but a child. What can I do?"

A moment before I had been cheerful, looking forward to seeing Washington, the Federal City of my dreams. All my born days, it seemed, I had tiptoed in with fresh candles at Montpelier, and heard my master and his friends talk about Washington City and the White House.

I took pride in being a slave child serving men and women who would be remembered in history. My own master, James Madison, was fourth president of our United States! When slaves at Montpelier met other slaves in Virginia, we let them know who we were. We looked down on them like pine trees over weeds.

And now I was on my way to Washington City to serve at the White House. But, would I be welcomed by my mistress?

Tobias stared off along the road. "You be needed to trim wicks, to whip ice cream, to fetch flowers from Market Square."

I heaved a sigh. "What more, Tobias?"

"That be good reasons," he said gruffly.

I glanced at him. Perspiration soaked his high collar. Tiny Tobias, my white-haired Tobias, seemed fearful and grieving. I had acted selfishly. Gently I touched his wrinkled hand.

"Those reasons are wholly good," I said. "But, what is the real reason, Tobias?"

He did not look at me, but I sensed that he felt more at peace. "You will learn, then you'll be understanding." He turned an ear to listen. "Even now," he said, nodding, "you will see our need."

Less than a hundred yards from where we sat, a road crossed ours. I listened and heard low moans, infants crying, and the clanking of metal chains.

Soon men, colored like myself, heads down, tramped the dusty road. A few boys within years of their manhood stumbled among them. Their hands were leather bound. In agony I stared and listened. Noisy chains trailed along the ground, shackling the leg of one slave to the leg of another slave. Some forty men passed in a pack, four to five slaves across. Now a wagon creaked into view. I wrung my hands for grief.

On the wagon were moaning women; children—boys and girls of my own age and size—staring fearfully; infants wailing in mothers' arms. They were packed body to body, standing and weaving, as horses drew the rusty wagon in jerks.

Tobias had moved not a cubit, but I felt myself rise from the seat. I could not bear the sight. Covering my eyes, I moaned. He snatched me down, and briefly touched my lips for me to be silent. Never before had I seen slaves driven to market. I could hardly believe my eyes.

My days at Montpelier had been spent in peaceful service as a proud house slave. Oh, the overseers caused suffering enough with floggings and other discipline. I heard other slaves' complaints late at night, but those complaints were not my concern. I thought slaves who ran away deserved to be punished. I was careful not to get caught when I didn't obey, and mostly I obeyed my master.

True, my mother, my father, both were taken from me. Sold away. I had barely known them. They worked on the plantation as field slaves; I worked in the master's mansion as a house slave.

Overseers sometimes marched humming field

slaves, rakes and hoes over their shoulders, past our huts. When I was small, Aunt Ruth, the woman who raised all the colored pickaninnies, would point and tell me, "Virginia, there be your mama. There be your papa."

I would stare at them with hungry eyes, with thirsting heart. I needed them, but knowing them was not to be, so I tried my best to ignore that hunger, that thirst. However, like missing a meal on a hard-work day, it left me faint and dizzy.

Then one night, a woman stole into Aunt Ruth's cabin. Rocking back and forth, she hugged me tightly. "I be your mama, Virginia," she whispered. "And know that you have a papa who loves you as well."

The next day they were sold away from me.

I was sleepy that night, but the close embrace, the rocking, the words, cheered my heart. In the strength of that mama-love, and in the strength of God's goodness, I had stumbled through my childhood days.

Yet, how I yearned for a mama, for a papa. I spent many hours thinking of them. Wondering where they were. Wondering if they were thinking of me. In my heart I clung to the strength in my mama's hug, the strength in my mama's words that night.

My mind had held that mother-father loss in a grieving hole in my heart. The traders' slaves before me opened up that hole.

Now, because of my moan, white men wearing riding breeches and carrying rifles galloped toward us. Tobias did not move. I settled myself and stared ahead as Tobias did. My face put on a mask of hide-feelings like his. So tightly did my hands clutch each other on my lap, that my fingers pained.

"You, African," yelled the first white man, brandishing his rifle, "what is your business? Show me your papers!"

My heart fluttered against my ribs like a caged bird beating its fragile wings against the bars. Tobias took a deep breath and moistened his lips.

"Our master be President James Madison of these United States," he said.

The slave traders rode around our chariot. They peered inside, where there were new day dresses for Miss Dolley and dimity curtains for the White House.

"Well," said the first man.

"So," said the second, and they rode away.

I sat all atremble, but I made not a sound. Those slave traders might have stolen me for selling. I had papers tucked in my dress telling my name, age, and owners, but what would papers mean on a deserted road?

When they passed, I bent my head to my knees, trembling. Next, I looked up into the green-leaf maple and gave thanks for our delivery. Tobias leaped down and began to hitch our horses. He turned his kindly gaze on me. "Watch well, Virginia."

I nodded and watched the order of attachment for hitching, just as on the trip I had learned the tricks of driving four horses. Would I need to know these things one day?

The suffering of those slaves on their way to market stung like salt in a wound. Would I help slaves like those? What did Tobias have in mind for me?

When he had climbed back into his seat, he asked: "Do you now understand about our people?"

"Yes," I whispered. My face, like his, wore the hide-feelings mask. Yes, I understood about my people.

Chapter Two

As we continued our journey, our frisky young horses seemed much refreshed from the grass and the watering. I was not accustomed to speak overly much, and Tobias was another person of silence.

Several times I saw Indians, brown like myself, peering out of the midst of trees. I touched his elbow and pointed to an Indian child whose straight black hair was in two braids. My thick hair required twelve braids; "Same as the twelve tribes of Israel," said Aunt Ruth back at Montpelier.

Aunt Ruth was not cruel, but then neither was she kind. She had no favorites among us. I always thought she hardened her heart so that our eventual sale wouldn't grieve her. I missed her, but I had not been sorry to leave her.

Beside us now this Indian child was bare of foot and dressed in a soft-looking leather dress. I smiled and she smiled back.

Tobias nodded. He would speak when he was ready. We drove on, the soft *clunk clunk* of our horses' hooves tapping the dusty road.

"Mostly Indians been got rid of," he said after a while. "They be tolerated less and less in Washington City. Some used to trade at Market Square."

"Indians got rid of?" I asked. This first day of August was opening my eyes to many things. There were Indians living in Virginia near Montpelier. I had played hide-and-go-seek with their children in the forest. "How got rid of?"

"Rounded up. Escorted west by soldiers. Made to march in winter cold or summer heat. Algonquins," he said.

I peered about for more Indian children, but saw none. Soon Tobias drew the horses to a stop. When I looked around, I saw only trees, but he pointed to a rock. "Go. Read to me."

I swung down and gingerly approached a small square stone set between two tree stumps. On it was inscribed: *The Boundry of the City*.

I gave a cry and clasped my hands. "The Boundry Stone," I called. "Is this the first one?"

Tobias smiled. "I don't know. The first one was set in April 1791, by General George Washington himself. But I know not if this be it." He scratched his knee. "Learn well, Virginia. Washington City be in a ten-mile square they call the Territory of Columbia. There be forty of these stones to mark it off. Any time you be lost and can find a stone, you know where you be."

Back to the chariot I waddled stiffly, but before climbing up I stood for a moment. A hidden bird burst forth in song, a grand melody for my first glimpse of a Boundry Stone to Washington City. Yet I felt fearful. Who could foretell what might happen when I reached the President's House?

As we rode on, not a soul nor a home appeared to announce the city. Then the chariot swayed as the four horses climbed a hill and stopped again, and this time we were overlooking the city.

Below was land green with treetops, watered by a sky blue river. On a far hill stood a building of white stone and red brick. A few brick homes dotted the streets, but twice as many homes were wooden, surrounded by scattered shacks and huts of wood. It seemed to me there were more streets than houses.

I spied a blaze of light amidst the green. Across the river was a large building gleaming wholly white. It shouted from the quiet of the green treetops. Spying it, I called: "The White House! Oh, it must be so. Tell me, Tobias?"

He nodded, and leaned back smiling. "Built of new stone, mighty white, and cut fresh from the quarry. That be the President's House."

For joy I hugged myself. Now everything seemed all right. "And, will I live there?" Pride bubbled within me. Slave child to the president of these United States!

"No," he said and laughed. "You be a worker there. You live in slave . . . accommodations." He said the word softly.

"Oh, hurry, hurry," I called. "We're almost there."

Paying me no mind, Tobias sat calm as a hen hatching chickens. There was more he wanted to show me. He pointed. "There be the Capitol Building set on Jenkins Hill." That was the building of white stone and red brick.

He smiled. "Every Easter Miss Dolley has set the custom of egg rolling on the Capitol grounds. Children—colored, white, even Indian—can roll their eggs on Capitol Hill."

I hugged myself and vowed not to miss egg rolling at Easter. Tobias started the chariot, the horses stepping even livelier than before, as if sensing they were close to home. We crossed the river on a wooden bridge where our horses' hooves made quite a clatter.

Each end of the bridge was set in huge mossy green stones. The blue river flowed prettily, its blue silvered by sunshine. It smelled fresh. Excitement made my heart dance within me.

"Potomac River," Tobias said. He pointed to the right. "Pay attention, Virginia. Eastern Branch meet with Anacostia River over there. You can take a boat from here to reach Alexandria most every hour of the day."

Farther on he pointed. "The Mall." It was a broad, dusty, east-west public place filled with stalls. It both smelled and sounded of squealing pigs and honking geese and braying donkeys. Cows wandered, munching any grass to be found. When a barking dog ran chasing a gander, a striped mother cat with her four tiger kittens scrambled under an empty wagon for safety.

"Wait," I called to Tobias.

Grinning now, he stopped. I swung stiffly down and peeked through the wheels of that wagon to where the mother cat sat surrounded by her kittens. No sooner than they saw me did they prance out to play. I sat back laughing, and caressed the silken fur of the tiger kits. The mother rubbed against my back, purring and seeming to beg for petting.

"Oh, Tobias," I called. "They love me."

He smiled.

When a man with a workman's cap and red cheeks whistled, all the cats but one left me. This kitten arched his back purring, and when I lifted him, he rubbed his soft silky head beneath my chin. He needed me.

"You want the kitten?" asked the man.

I nodded, holding my breath.

"Keep it. But, care well for it."

"I will, I will," I called, and I scrambled back on the Madison chariot-and-four. Could I keep a kitten? Many cats and kittens lived at Montpelier, but I had never owned one. What would Tobias say?

He only smiled. As I gazed at him, he glanced ahead; his smile quickly changed to a grimace and then to the mask. We had passed wooden pens where all manner of animals—pigs, goats, geese—were kept. Now I saw a pen where slaves were kept. People, out in hot sunlight, huddled and held in chains. I had heard that slaves in transport were kept starved and thirsty so as not to have the strength to escape or rebel. It was "breaking them in," part of discipline. Now I saw for myself.

White men selling slaves gestured toward a slave standing outside the pen. His leg was chained to a stump; his mouth hung open. His tongue lolled about as he swayed in the heat. His thirst screamed out to me, and I burned in anger.

Pressing my tiger kitten into Tobias's arms, I leaped clumsily off the chariot seat. Nearby a woman carried a water pitcher and I snatched it from her.

"He needs water!" I yelled at her. I lumbered over to hold the pitcher to the man's lips. He sucked the water noisily.

After he drank, I returned the pitcher to the angry woman. She shook her fist at me, but I swung up on the chariot, took my kitten back, and Tobias started the horses trotting rapidly away.

Oh, the suffering of slavery. As if a fog had cleared, how apparent that suffering had become to me that first day of August.

At that moment I named my little tiger kitten the loveliest word I knew. Liberty!

Chapter Three

As if nothing had happened, Tobias said: "There be twenty-five good springs for drinking water in Washington City. You'll learn where they be." The horses trotted on.

I nodded and petted my kitten. Good, kind Tobias, he didn't scold me for giving the man water. Small wonder he hadn't done it himself, though he would have received forty lashes, which could kill a hunchback like him. Children could get away with some things as slaves. At Montpelier if children were caught stealing apples, they were scolded. If grown-ups were caught, they were flogged.

Tobias pointed. "Learn well. You'll need to know.

From White House to Capitol be about a mile and a half."

Pigs and geese wandered streets well marked but dusty and rutted. The streets were far worse than the clean cobblestone streets we had passed over in Alexandria and in other towns in Virginia. Tobias bade me notice that Washington City streets were numbered in the east-west direction, and marked in alphabetical letters in the north-south direction.

He pointed. "There be Market Square. They hold market on Tuesdays, Thursdays, and Saturdays. You be going thereabouts many times."

The weeds were trampled in a two-block area between Seventh and Ninth streets on Pennsylvania Avenue. The smell of rotten vegetables and fermenting fruits tickled my nose. Some few sheds and stalls stood empty under the burning sun. Tomorrow would be a market day; I hoped I could go to buy with someone.

"What will I buy?"

"Eggs, or ham, or butter, or fruit, or flowers."

"Don't they have hens and gardens at the White House?"

Tobias laughed. "President's House ain't no plantation nor farm, Virginia. They buy they food."

Liberty Kitty had dozed off on my lap. That was proof he was happy with me. How I loved that tiger kitten, a

18

silken puff of fur. No longer all alone, I could hug and love my kitten.

Along side streets I saw a few taverns, inns, and warehouses. Broad avenues cut across numbered and lettered streets. "Avenues," said Tobias, as if reading my thoughts, "are named for our fifteen states of the United States."

Pennsylvania Avenue, although dusty and rutted, was surely the grandest of them all. It had a footpath on either side. Broad with three lanes, it grew a guard of sentinel poplars. Now I rode down that avenue between the straight lofty trees, and my heart beat proudly in my chest.

Ahead I saw the sparkling white of our President's House. But before we reached it, I needed to know what Tobias had planned for me. What was my secret work? How could I help other slaves?

I slapped the hard wooden seat. "What do you have in mind for me, Tobias? I won't tell, that you know."

Silent, Tobias didn't tell me what I had to do.

I tried to guess. "Escape is not ofttimes successful for slaves," said I.

Bent forward, Tobias began whispering. "It be successful when British ships need sailors, seamen black or white. It be successful by water when they be searching land. It be successful when them British take slaves to the West Indies to live." He straightened up.

Those words reminded me of something. The day before we left I had heard a white man complain that the British were "stealing" American slaves. Peace commissioners were to demand that the British return them. The British and the War of 1812 were means of our escape. Now I knew!

"There," said Tobias louder, as if he had said nothing before, "that building to the east of the White House be the Treasury Building; that building to the west be the War Office. You might be sent with messages."

I stared at the buildings, but mostly at the White House.

The President's House was wide. I counted ten windows across the front, and there was a central door behind a shallow porch they called a portico. The house was two stories high plus a basement and attic; and the roof had many chimneys. The yard was no grassy lawn, but rocky with few trees and those not fancy. Opposite the south portico I knew there was a north portico; and there were east and west terraces.

The Virginia estate I had worked at, Montpelier, was prettier to my way of thinking. And yet, because it was the President's House in the Federal City, my heart began to frolic for joy. Washington was a city of promise.

As we *clip-clopped* closer to the President's House, I

saw another carriage pull up with a visitor. Slaves opened the door of the President's House, ran out, and assisted a lady to descend. From her visits to Montpelier, I knew Mrs. Anna Cutts, sister of Mrs. Dolley Madison.

And now Miss Dolley herself tripped out in a pretty day dress of cool lavender with lacy lavender cap to match. Our rosy-faced mistress was plump and tall, taller by three to four inches than our master. When she spied her chariot-and-four, she took her sister's hand and strolled over to us.

"Tobias," she said, her blue eyes twinkling, "welcome home. Do you have my new dresses?" She turned to her sister. "Anna, dearest, you should see what my dressmaker has sewed for me in the style of Paris, and one or two for you.

"But, who is this?" she asked, noticing me for the first time.

I slid down and curtsied before them. I knew Miss Dolley would recognize me. Her memory for faces and names was legendary.

"Why this is Virgie from Montpelier," she said. Turning to her sister, she added, "Her name is Virginia, but since that name is unbecoming for a slave child, I call her Virgie."

"Why unbecoming, Dolley dear?" asked Mrs. Cutts.

"We are Virginians," said Miss Dolley, with a toss of her head. "We can't allow a colored child to be named Virginia."

I thought: Who says it's unbecoming for a colored child to be named Virginia? My mother gave me my name, not you. And, when I am at liberty in the West Indies, I shall scream out my name every day. Virginia, Virginia! My name is Virginia!

I clasped Liberty Kitty too tightly. He meowed protest from my arms. With another curtsy, I took a step aside, but Miss Dolley caught my arm. "So, Virgie, why have you come?"

Again Liberty Kitty meowed protest. What could I answer?

Chapter Four

If I kept my silence, would Tobias speak for me? To avoid Miss Dolley's gaze, I glanced away. Tobias looked at the rocky dirt, his face a mask.

"Virgie, I order you to speak," said Miss Dolley. With her lacy handkerchief she dabbed perspiration from her forehead.

"I came to work . . . at parties . . . to trim wicks, to whip ice cream, to fetch flowers from Market Square." I backed away and squeezed Liberty Kitty so tightly he scratched me and bit my elbow.

Mrs. Cutts lifted her gloved hand to her forehead and said, "Let us get out of this cruel sunlight, dearest Dolley."

But Miss Dolley looked deeply into my eyes. "Why do you now limp, Virgie?"

She hadn't seen me since January. "I had an accident, ma'am." It was a deliberate accident. "But, I can work."

With a sigh she said, "Then go work, Virgie. Tell Aunt Sally in the kitchen I have sent you."

She had said nothing about Liberty Kitty. Again I curtsied, and walked toward the side of the President's House. Relief washed over me like a cooling shower in summer.

"No, Virgie," called my mistress, stepping ahead and leaving me behind. "Introduce yourself to Monsieur Sioussant. Go in the front door." She and her sister hastened to the house.

Turning, I watched slave women pass me carrying clothes and curtains from our chariot. After a while I followed one, but she turned and walked behind me. She stepped on my heels and almost made me stumble. Was I too slow? Was I in her way? Petting Liberty Kitty, I walked faster. Again she stepped on my heels, and bumped me in the rear. My heart was racing. I tried to walk faster still, but she was fast as well. Another passing slave woman giggled.

I felt embarrassed, ashamed. What was I doing wrong?

When we reached the portico steps leading up to the White House door, that bumping woman shoved me to fall on my face. Liberty Kitty jumped from my arms. Stones hurt my hands and knees. I sat and picked up Liberty Kitty, then looked into that woman's grin. She kicked my ankle.

"Go work, Virgie," she said, mimicking Miss Dolley.

Others passed us smiling. Was this some manner of greeting used in Washington City? Was I so countrified that I didn't understand? As I tried to rise from the steps, she kicked me again. What had I done to her?

Suddenly anger sizzled inside me. Manners were manners and meanness was meanness. This woman chose to be mean, and I knew how to make return. My face felt flushed, and I was breathless. Liberty Kitty I secured firmly under my arm. Then, lips pressed together tightly, I waited. When that woman swung her foot to kick me again, I caught her ankle and jerked.

She fell on her back with a thump and a scream. Miss Dolley's curtains scattered in the dust. Good, I thought. Served that woman right!

Arising, I marched up the steps with head high and shoulders stiff. But inside I felt sad. Why was that woman cruel to me? Would everyone be like that?

Miss Dolley and her sister had disappeared. A tall white man who had viewed it all smiled at me. He wore white stockings with brown pantaloons and a day shirt of white silk.

"I am Monsieur Jean Pierre Sioussant," he said bowing. "Zere are zome who call me French John. And zat"— he pointed out the door where the woman scrambled to pick up her armful— "zat is Rosetta Bell. And you?"

I curtsied and said, "My name is Virginia of Madison, but Miss Dolley calls me Virgie."

"Welcome, Virginia," he said, and waved behind him at rooms. "Look wherever it pleezes you. I must now go remind Madame Madison of her appointments for tomorrow."

I wandered in, patting Liberty Kitty. Now that I had made an enemy, I would have to beware. The lovely sight before me lost its brilliance. Yet I could see that the foyer was truly grand, with large fine staircase, deep carpets, and portraits in gilded frames. General George Washington's portrait attracted my eye.

Our first president stood tall, a drawn sword in his left hand, and his right hand extended over a table. Of course, he was in a white powdered wig.

Glancing over my shoulder, I hastened on before that woman, Rosetta Bell, entered. In the far rear the kitchen was abustle with about seven servants and the sound of clattering, clinking chinaware. The smell of rising bread and roasting chicken bid my spirits soar. I glanced around quickly.

However, I was greatly disappointed. None of the

kitchen servants looked familiar. I had thought I would find old friends. For years, when slaves were carried off by the overseer, I thought they had gone to Washington City to work for our master. I had been wrong. Every face there was new.

"Aunt Sally?" I asked softly.

A tall, thin, brown woman in a white turban and wearing an apron over a yellow dress turned to stare at me. "Honey child, what you be doing in here?"

"Mistress Madison sent me to you," I said. "I am Virginia of Madison. Tobias brought me from Montpelier."

Aunt Sally raised both arms and hastened to embrace me.

"Virginia, we been expecting you," she whispered. "Honey child, you be needing a refreshing bath after that long trip. How you be, child?" She dragged me out the door. Stiff-legged and curious, I tried to keep up with her.

She gestured to a girl. "Prisca, fetch soap, and seek those clothes we been saving for Virginia." Prisca, a light-skinned slave about my age with blue-gray eyes, smiled and skipped away.

Aunt Sally allowed as how I could bathe in her slave hut, a small wooden shanty in back of the White House. A round wooden tub was filled with water slightly warm. She washed and rinsed my hair. Once combed into my twelve braids, I could care for it myself, braid by braid. After my bath, she bid me lie on my stomach and she rubbed bacon fat on my scarred backsides and legs. Prisca came in and gave a cry when she saw the scars.

The grease felt soothing; Aunt Sally was helping me heal. I realized my story had spread to Washington.

"Child, be I hurting you?" Aunt Sally asked.

"No, ma'am."

Prisca stood staring.

"Be any of them near?" asked Aunt Sally.

Prisca glanced outside the small shanty that was one room with two doors. "No, Aunt Sally."

I dressed. As she braided my hair, Aunt Sally said, "Tell Prisca how your legs be painful scarred."

I was pleased that Prisca would learn about my bravery.

I began: "Christmas week as usual we had good victuals to eat at Montpelier, but in January the overseer withheld food. He said he didn't want us to get uppity. We were all sorely hungry, almost too weak to work, and one night . . . someone"— I didn't tell his name because he was still at Montpelier— "someone stole three chickens.

"They brought a big soup pot from the mansion kitchen and set the chickens to cook over the fire. About twenty of us slaves were gathered in a shed to eat, and it was the cold of the night. Not one of us made a sound."

Prisca kept bobbing out the doorway to look around. At one time she tapped her sandal three times, and Aunt Sally said, "Honey child, we'll show you all the chinaware. You'll . . ."

When Prisca nodded, Aunt Sally said, "Go on. There's those that can know, and those that can't. Be that clear?"

I nodded, but I felt confused. How would I know them apart?

I went on: "Then the overseer shook the locked door. We hadn't heard his footsteps. Someone" — again I didn't tell names— "lifted the pot off the fire by handles and carried it to a corner of the room." In spite of August heat, I shuddered.

"Go on, honey child."

"The overseer had his gun. Behind him stood another white man carrying leather thongs for binding wrists. We answered all his questions. Then he saw the soup pot. If he had found three chickens stolen, our men and women would have been flogged and sold; we children punished by more hunger.

" 'Why is the soup pot here?' asked the overseer.

"I had been tossing stones with a boy. With stone in hand I stood.

" 'I been cutting seasonings for the master's stew

tomorrow,' someone said, and she showed him onions for our chicken soup. I felt frantic. Someone had to do something, but no one was moving. How could I keep him from opening that soup pot?

"Still tossing the stone, I skipped over. I sat on the pot. Through my skirt the heat burned my backsides. Burned my legs. I just tossed and caught my stone. I think I even smiled.

"The overseer stared at me.

"The steam burned, so I jiggled until the top closed tightly. The heat . . . was most painful."

My tears now rolled. Aunt Sally kissed me on the crown of my head. "But," I went on, "the overseer and the other man left. We stayed still for a time. My legs were sorely painful. As we expected, he popped back in. Still, I sat and tossed my stone. Then the overseer left, and we heard him ride away on a horse.

"I began to cry. Two people had to lift me off the soup pot. I couldn't move myself. They said my backsides and legs were red and blistered. Aunt Ruth applied snow to cool the burn. Now the pain is only a pulling stiffness of the scars."

Aunt Sally told Prisca, "With bacon grease we fighting scars that could cripple her. Got to keep her legs stretched."

I looked for my kitten. In the corner Liberty Kitty

daintily ate an oyster Aunt Sally had given him. He had cool water in a fine teacup with a broken handle.

I wondered: What made me brave sometimes and silly other times? Was I now a steadfast girl?

Prisca had tears rolling down her pretty cheeks. She nodded and tapped her sandal three times. Rosetta Bell peered in the door, stared at Liberty Kitty, grinned, and walked on. I ran and picked up my kitty. Why did that woman treat me mean? I had done nothing to her. I hoped she wouldn't harm my kitten.

Chapter Five

That night there was a storm of noises from dogs barking, cats fighting, and geese, pigs, and cows wandering Washington City streets. However, I slept soundly in a hut with Prisca and two older women. Unsightly servants' quarters—shacks and slave huts—in back of the President's House were most improper, I thought.

Next morning Miss Dolley was up at an early hour ordering her household of servants and slaves, blacks and whites. While Tobias and I and several others belonged to the master, many slaves were hired out from city owners. A few White House servants were freedmen; they worked for their own hire.

Before dawn someone had showed me how to tote water for drinking from a spring many blocks away. For the job I had a water wagon. Then later, while some were cleaning rooms, or washing the master's underwear and shirts, I worked in the kitchen with Aunt Sally.

In the kitchen there was great joking. Prisca could wrinkle her face like the master, and say, "Mrs. Madison, may I have a word with you, please?" Her tone of voice and space of words were just like the master's. Everyone choked, laughing silently, so as not to be heard by the mistress.

There was a high-minded washerwoman who upon entering the kitchen swished her long skirt around the food tables. Prisca kept us all giggling when she swished her skirt in imitation.

Even before breakfast that first morning, Aunt Sally turned to me. "Let me show you the White House china, Virginia." We went into a large room, a china closet.

She held out a dish with design of black lines on white. An angel with trumpet was in the center, and the dish edges were wavy. "We has a few of these from President George Washington's time.

"Miss Dolley ofttimes requests small breakfast groupings on these." Aunt Sally held blue-and-white dishes with a landscape scene and flowered border.

"These belonged to Mrs. Abigail Adams." This was history of a new nation. I breathed deeply.

"Miss Abigail, she loved blue dishes." Aunt Sally touched my arm and pointed to other blue dishes. "Master Thomas Jefferson ordered blue chinaware from China too."

When she tapped one with a spoon, it rang like a bell. How thin and lovely. How likely to break! I trembled and hoped I wouldn't get in trouble for breaking dishes.

Next I recognized our master's white dishes with fluted edges. There were also Madison dishes with an orange border and a design in shapes of black and gold.

Out of the corner of my eye I spied Liberty Kitty chasing his fluffy tiger tail. He had followed me.

"Now, you must learn these," Aunt Sally said. "When I send you in here for dishes, there be egg dishes, chocolate dishes"— she pointed— "cream pots, flowerpots, confection dishes, butter boats, square stew dishes, porringers with these covers, mustard pots, sugar dishes, ice plates, platters, pudding dishes. . . ."

My head spun like a muddy wagon wheel. I pointed to a lovely basketlike dish on a pedestal.

"China fruit basket," said Aunt Sally.

• • •

My chinaware lesson was put to test in a short time. I soon carried hot tea into the breakfast room and placed the silver pot on a silver serving tray.

The Madisons had many houseguests, same as at Montpelier. Besides about twenty adults, there were five children at breakfast. Other slaves served them. In fact, one family had two slaves of their own attending them. None of the white children would look at me.

I watched the white mothers with their children. Would my mother have told me to eat nicely? Would she have kissed my cheek? Would she have smoothed down my collar? I reached for my collar, and it did need straightening. I almost cried right then and there. As a child, did I not deserve a mother?

For breakfast the Madisons and guests had the following food: tea, coffee, muffins, hot wheat bread, hot corn bread, cold ham, a warm pone or corn loaf, steaming hashes, and chicken. How good it all smelled. They also were offered on the sideboard the following: pineapples, cakes, nuts, and figs.

Miss Dolley stood by a houseguest. "Virgie," she called, "fetch a mustard pot to flavor the ham."

I stared at the orange-and-black chinaware they were using for breakfast, and I ran. In the china closet I found a mustard pot to match. I filled it in the kitchen.

Returning triumphant, I felt proud of myself. How quickly I worked. I knew just what pot to use. Surely my mistress would praise me?

By the time I returned, however, Miss Dolley had hastened to the master who stood in the doorway. "Mr. Madison, be not anxious," she whispered, "many do agree with you."

His answer I did not hear, but from his posture he seemed low in spirits. He held both her hands in his. I passed holding the mustard pot. No one paid any attention to me as I put my mustard pot next to the ham. My master had not even noticed I was there.

Miss Dolley told him, "While you are in with the men, I will speak to their wives. Whereas the husbands may not understand the need to compromise, the wives will listen to your wisdom. Worry not." He seemed sorry to leave her. After a squeeze of hands, he turned away with head higher than before.

Master James Madison was short and skinny. Even so they said he was mighty in knowledge, and was known as the philosopher of the Constitution. He was nearly twenty years older than our mistress; he was in his sixties, she in her forties. He proved a kindly, mild, and temperate master, and I always tried to please him. Neither of the Madisons was given to cruelty with slaves; they hired an overseer for that.

Our master called, "Remember, my cabinet this noon."

Miss Dolley murmured something, then caught sight of me with ears full sail. "Virgie," she said, "tell Monsieur Jean Pierre to cancel my appointment at the orphanage for this afternoon. And tell Aunt Sally we'll be having a dove party."

I curtsied and ran out. On my way to the kitchen I heard someone grunt as she walked behind me in the wide White House hall. Servants coming toward me covered their mouths in laughter. Glancing back, I saw Rosetta Bell stiff-walking to imitate me.

Why would she do that? What did she have against me? Every time I saw her she hurt my feelings. I stuffed my hurt feelings in that grieving hole in my heart until it was likely to explode!

When I told French John about the dove party, he raised eyes heavenward, sighed, and hastened away. Aunt Sally clapped to get attention. Servants bustled at her announcement.

"We feed doves and other birds at Montpelier," I told Aunt Sally, "but only in the winter."

Suddenly everyone in the kitchen began to laugh. "Dove party. She think we is about to be feeding birds," said a woman. And they laughed harder. Face warm, I stared at the floor. How could I understand if no one told me?

"Dove parties be for cabinet wives," someone said. "While the cabinet members meet downstairs, their wives have a dove party upstairs with Miss Dolley."

It was almost noon on Tuesday, August 2, 1814.

"You, Virginia and Prisca, get your baskets and run to market for me," called Aunt Sally. Swallowing my embarrassment, I took off my apron.

Now I would see Market Square.

Chapter Six

A slave named Clementine walked with Prisca and myself on the hot dusty avenue to Market Square. "I be going to fetch candles for tomorrow's drawing room," Clementine said. She was old, maybe thirty, but still pretty.

Turning a corner near us, a moaning group of slaves, bound and chained, dragged bare feet in the dust. Because I had no food or drink to give them, I felt frantic at first, but then I remembered Tobias's plan. *We have a secret plan, and we will save you,* sang my heart.

But my face wore the mask, as did the faces of Prisca and Clementine. My secret tickled to be told, but I kept silent.

When Clementine started to leave us, she caught my arm and pulled me to stand by Prisca. "See how white and pretty she be?" asked Clementine, holding Prisca's fair-skinned arm by my brown one.

"Virginia, wear your hat to shade your face, and pull long sleeves down. Maybe you get lighter too. Prisca, she be nearly white." Clementine pulled Prisca's hat brim to shade her face in the burning sun. "Ain't nobody love black."

With that, Clementine bustled off toward her candle shop.

Nobody loved black? I loved black. Those black slaves were my people. In defiance I pushed my hat to hang down my back, and shoved my sleeves up to expose my brown arms to sunlight. Prisca glanced away, and I saw her wince.

Market Square was smelly, crowded, and noisy. There seemed no order. Vendors sold squawking chickens, goat meat, eggs, butter, greens, beans, flowers. We were there for flowers.

Prisca chose the vendor, selected the blooms, and paid. "Give us a water bucket," she asked. "The flowers must stay fresh. We'll return it."

That was all very well, but she shoved that bucket at me to carry. It was heavy with water, pink roses, yellow lilies, and red and white geraniums. Prisca marched ahead, and I was left limping in her dust.

In the bright, hot August sunlight the dusty streets smelled of horse manure. Big bluebottle flies buzzed over the horse droppings. Insects droned a sleepy song of summer heat.

"Prisca," I called. She waited for me. Breathing hard, I set the bucket down. "Why did you leave me?"

"Because you don't like my fair skin," she said, with a toss of her head.

"Here," I told her, "carry this bucket. Fear not, I like your fair skin. Don't I have the right to like my brown skin as well?" That seemed to ease her feelings, and she began to chat.

"Watch out for that Clementine. She tell a lie on you in a minute, 'specially to save her own hide."

"What about Rosetta Bell?" I asked.

"Her child done just what you be doing for the mistress. She mad about that." I didn't understand, but Prisca went on.

"Too bad these streets ain't paved, swept, or lighted 'cause they ain't got the money." A pile of straw blocked our path and we trod around it.

"I know."

"This here war," she said, "it's taking all our money, and it ain't our master's fault. He be influenced by them young congressmen called War Hawks. You know?"

I nodded.

Prisca giggled. She seemed to enjoy telling me

things. "You know a black man, an astronomer, he survey and lay out these here streets. He have the name of Benjamin Banneker."

I hadn't learned that at Montpelier.

"You interested in going to school?" she asked.

"School?" I asked. "For a colored child?"

"Run by coloreds for coloreds. There's some fine colored folks hereabouts. Ain't nobody need be dumb in Washington City."

When we trotted into the kitchen, Aunt Sally was fit to be tied. "Dillydallying when we need them flowers!" she said. "Virginia, cut flowers low for flower bowls on the table. Don't mix no colors now. And be quick about it, honey child."

I was sorry we had taken so long, but it was fun listening to Prisca. Clementine had already returned, and she showed me how to arrange blossoms in china bowls. When I carried them upstairs, I gasped.

The small room for the dove party was beautiful. In a corner someone played a piano, and someone else a guitar. There were yellow drapes and carpet; a table set in white china with fluted edges; ladies sitting on brocaded yellow couches; ladies on fine, yellow damask-covered chairs. And mirrors on two walls made the cozy room seem larger.

Tiptoeing in, I liked how I looked in those mirrors. Turning this way and that, I saw my twelve bushy braids; my green dress and white apron were neatly starched and ironed. Already I had new clothes. We slaves wore some fine clothes at the President's House! And I hadn't been hungry.

With care, I began placing flower bowls in the centers of three tables. My spirits grew so cheerful I stuck a white rose stem in one of my braids.

The tables had plates set with a napkin under each plate. Although the ladies had not yet come to table, I saw platters of roast beef, cold veal, pease porridge, and a fluffy dessert of Indian pudding. There were also tea and coffee, figs, nuts, and pineapple.

I dared not taste a bit. Maybe the ladies wouldn't eat it all? Maybe I could clear the trays later? I licked my lips.

Sukey, Miss Dolley's personal maid, walked in, looked around, and left. I think she counted to see if everyone was there. Downstairs Miss Dolley had been greeting the cabinet wives as John Freeman, the colored doorman, let the couples in.

Now Mrs. Dolley Payne Todd Madison—Aunt Ruth always called her by all her names—made her entrance. Aunt Ruth said Miss Dolley never walked in, she "made an entrance"!

All the wives wore hats, but our mistress wore feathery turbans over her sleek black hair. The pink turban she wore this day was fastened by a crescent moon, and waved two peacock feathers. Her low-cut gown was a matching rose pink and simple—no ruffles. And she wore no jewelry for this day affair.

Miss Dolley glanced over the tables and smiled. Murmuring each cabinet wife's name in turn, she greeted them again and began checking the tables.

Then she spied me. With flower tray in hand, I was melting myself away like snow on a sunny rooftop. Miss Dolley snatched the rose out of my hair.

"Virgie," she scolded softly, "it is unbecoming for you to wear a flower in your hair."

Silently I stared at her, knowing I should have said, Yes, ma'am. I think my face was sullen, as Aunt Ruth would say. Not wear flowers in my hair? Well, when I was at liberty in the West Indies, I would wear a flower in my hair every day. I promised myself.

"And," she said, waving at my head, "your hair is much too long and much too thick. Either cut it off, or . . ." She pulled a string from a small bag. "Here."

My busy mistress turned from her guests and took the time to tie my braids together. Now they hung like a bundle of hay at the back of my neck. She had noticed me; she had touched me. I felt happy then. Glancing in the mirror, I liked it. I curtsied and stumbled out of the room.

Ahead of me, serving women had raced away to tell all the kitchen staff the bad news that Miss Dolley was displeased with me. How they devoured bad news. By the time I reached the kitchen, they were all amurmur.

"Oh, honey child," said Aunt Sally, and she patted my shoulder. Her face wore fright and sadness.

They had not seen my mistress tie back my braids. I felt so pleased that she had taken the time to fix my braids I quickly showed Aunt Sally what she had done.

Chapter Seven

The next day was Wednesday, August 3. Every Wednesday Mrs. Dolley Madison held a drawing room. There were no invitations. As Aunt Sally said, "Everybody who be anybody know to come."

I had known the drawing room at Montpelier. Now I was eager to see the drawing room at the White House.

All Wednesday between meals was spent in preparation. It was both summer heat and excitement that set the kitchen aflame. Everything smelled rich and flavorful. Flowers from the dove party had been cooled in the White House basement. Now, without looking at them very closely, I carried the tray of flowers down the hall to where French John checked everything.

"Wait, Virgie," said French John. "Non, non, zese will not be zuitable." He groaned and looked heavenward. Having watched him look to heaven before, I wondered if he had a dead friend up there.

Miss Dolley strode up behind him. She picked over the flowers and lifted a wilted petal on her finger. "Monsieur is correct. Virgie, why have you poured the water out?"

I stared. When I had placed those flower bowls in the basement, there had been water aplenty in each. I stared at the bowls, my mouth hung open. Yesterday there had been water, but now . . . My mind flew to Rosetta Bell like an arrow. Had she dumped the water? I knew better than to defend myself. No one was allowed to talk back.

Miss Dolley clasped her hands. "These flowers are dead. Garlands of greenery. Go, go. Quick, quick. Greenery will be suitable, don't you think, Monsieur Jean Pierre?"

"Yesss, Madame," he said with a hiss like a French snake, "zat will be zuitable."

I trod away. Where was I to find garlands of greenery, and quick? In the kitchen I set down the tray of flower bowls.

"Virgie," Clementine called, "I need you to whip this ice cream."

"Virgie," said Aunt Sally, "fetch me the butter boats." For a brief moment, I stood, mouth open.

"No, no," I called. "I must seek garlands of greenery." I felt frantic. All at once everyone needed my help.

Liberty Kitty dozed by his teacup filled with creamy milk. He was pet of all the servants, and so far no one had stopped him from being there. I picked him up, put him in a basket, and ran outside.

"Liberty," I whispered, petting his silky fur, "we'll be in the West Indies one day soon. And then I won't need to seek garlands of greenery. Life will be easy there." He arched his back to my caress, and rubbed his head against my chin. He smelled of sour milk on whiskers, a nice kitten smell.

I scampered away and down to the bushes by Tiber Creek. Were any leaves suitable—zuitable, as French John said? I wandered staring. Pungent branches scratched my bare arms. Summer heat made the bushes smell good.

Ah, shiny green holly leaves, they wouldn't wilt easily. I began to cut them, but Liberty jumped from the basket. He didn't like sharing it with sticky leaves.

The basket full, I rested by the edge of the creek. As I sat, I stretched my legs against the scars' pull. Liberty

Kitty playfully swatted at an orange dragonfly by the water's edge.

Skirts swishing nearby caught my attention. I stood slowly, then bent over. It was Rosetta Bell and another slave woman. They seemed to be staring around at the bushes. Were they looking for me?

What if Rosetta knocked me into the creek and I drowned? What if she brought harm to Liberty Kitty? My heart was pounding, my legs were weak as wilted petals.

The leaves I had gathered were sufficient for many tables, but I needed to get back to the White House. How could I escape them?

That they were up to no good was apparent from their whispers and giggling. Why didn't they like me? Why did they make fun of me? No matter, I would soon be at liberty in the West Indies.

Wiggling my fingers silently, I caught my kitten's attention. At least he loved me. Step over step he moved to my grasp. Such a warm furry ball he was. I covered the sticky leaves with my apron and set him on them. Now, to escape!

The bushes were so thick by the creek's bank that to break out would be noisy. I couldn't outrun Rosetta Bell and her friend, not yet. I fingered a pebble, then chose several. My legs were stiff, but my arms were strong, and I had good aim.

When Rosetta had passed far enough to give me a chance to beat them running, I stood silently. With my best aim, I threw all the pebbles. They rattled far ahead of the women. As they ran toward the sound, I snatched my basket. Liberty Kitten and I scrambled silently along Tiber Creek's bank until I could break through to run to the White House.

I escaped Rosetta Bell, and Miss Dolley was satisfied with the "garlands of greenery." Others arranged the greenery while I was ordered to alternate salt and ice, just so in a tub, to make ice cream.

Beside me Aunt Sally stood forming small almond cakes for the oven. "Oh, don't Miss Dolley serve some fine food," she said in a low voice. "But it be Master Jefferson who done brought fancy food like ice cream here. He brought waffles, macaroni, vanilla, figs, raisins, almonds. And mustard, vinegar, oils. And anchovies. Fine wines. Honey child, you missed working in the kitchen when Master Thomas Jefferson be president."

"Whose slave are you, Aunt Sally?" I asked.

"A family of Wilsons hire me out. My old master died, and his son hire me out now. I been working here since Abigail and John Quincy Adams moved in back in November 1800."

She placed her cakes on a pan. "And Master Jefferson set up free schools for poor white children in Washington City. 'Course we got our own some too."

"I want to go to school," I said quickly. "Prisca told me about it." At Montpelier they taught me to read enough to understand directions, and to write a little, but there was much I needed to learn.

"Let me be thinking on that," said Aunt Sally.

Then while I put salt on ice, she allowed me to pick from dishes and taste a bit of everything: sweet raisins, crunchy almonds, juicy berries. Tobias was right, I did love the parties.

The Marine Band played in the foyer where our master and mistress had been greeting guests for the drawing room. I had heard the same music at Montpelier. My feet were set to dancing by melodies such as "Yankee Doodle" and marches such as "Jefferson's March." While working next to Aunt Sally in the kitchen, I was dancing like a stiff prancing pony.

For an hour or more carriages had been backed up on Pennsylvania Avenue. Each coach let guests out to ascend the stairs to the President's House before parking. They had played "Jefferson's March" before; now the band struck up "Madison's March." I knew the march melodies from Montpelier.

"What are they doing now?" I asked Aunt Sally. I hadn't yet seen the Oval Room, where Miss Dolley's drawing room was held.

"It be likely they all here now," said Aunt Sally. "French John, he done ordered the music for the Madisons to enter the drawing room. Some two, three hundred people come every Wednesday. Everybody who be anybody, and anybody who want to be somebody, know to come."

If it was possible for a slave child to be spoiled in three days, Aunt Sally and Tobias were spoiling me. Every day they did something nice for me, and for Prisca too. Now, I had begun to ask for favors. I tapped my feet to the march. "Can't I see, Aunt Sally? Send me up there, please, please, please?"

Chapter Eight

The music was delightful. Excitement danced with
me in the air, but the summer's heat was nearly intol-
erable. On my way upstairs behind Clementine I
paused to draw a breath of air from a front window.
In the summer's lavender dusk coachmen stood in
groups chatting; their coaches and patient horses were
parked up and down Pennsylvania Avenue.

And then I heard them; they dragged and bounced
their chains along the rutted soil on Pennsylvania
Avenue right past the very house of the president. Oh,
how cruel! Behind me plump, bright-eyed white faces;
before me sunken-cheeked, hungry, thirsty black faces.
These were my people suffering. Sorrow and anger

wrestled within me. What was the plan Tobias knew? When was I to be of help? My heart seemed ready to explode.

Clementine glanced out the window over my shoulder. "Don't be looking at the likes of them," she said. "Come on."

Seeing the trader slaves outside had dimmed my spirits, but the Oval Room was ablaze with candles and torches. Drapes were of golden-yellow satin. Mirrors on all walls extended the blazing splendor. A sunburst screen in yellow damask adorned the fireplace, and a beaming Miss Dolley and our short, sad-faced, wrinkled master stood there.

Wearing low-cut gowns, ladies were powdered and perfumed as weapons against the heat. Men wore black jackets with waistcoats, black pantaloons, and white silk stockings. Some wore powdered wigs. What a fickle girl I was. Soon I forgot the suffering slaves, and my chest swelled in pride. I was serving the most important people in the world!

Our mistress glowed in a simple low-cut gown of yellow satin with a white satin train that swept the floor for several yards. A gold necklace graced her lovely throat, and she wore bracelets to match. Her white silk turban waved a plume of white ostrich feathers. She flitted from person to person like a butterfly visiting flowers, and I limped with head high in admiration.

Miss Dolley wasn't pretty, but her gracious airs made her beautiful. If only I could be like her, I thought!

"Dear," she told a friend, "bring your widowed aunt here. We have single judges and congressmen aplenty. I'll find a husband for her." I had heard that Washington City was a place for matchmaking. I giggled.

As I trimmed wicks, two women spoke. "It's in the night hours that I worry most," said one. "Suppose the Negroes come to kill us in our sleep? Since they run the house, they have keys to lock the doors at night and open them by day."

"You can't treat slaves kindly because they become uppity and think well of themselves," said her friend. "But I fear to have them whipped too frequently." She sighed. "On our plantation the overseer deals with these things, and rather harshly, may I say."

Another woman leaned toward them. "A slave uprising is everyone's dread," she whispered.

At this, I felt spiteful; I remembered the slaves outside. So white people were afraid of us. We were their slaves. Threats, insults, and whippings kept us obedient. Yet they were afraid of us. As Aunt Ruth used to say, "If you beat a dog, watch out for his bite!"

Moving on, I overheard a man say, "Now that the British have defeated Napoleon, we're next. They could make us a colony again." He frowned.

Another man glanced at President Madison and

said, "He dared declare a war without fleets, without armies, and without money in the treasury. Thanks to 'Mr. Madison's war' we are now enemies of our mother country." He crossed his arms.

Clearly some people were displeased with our master as president. I hadn't known that. At Montpelier none of the slaves knew that. As I listened I thought: Master is only a servant just as I am a servant!

Just then Miss Dolley sailed past me, her train flowing behind her. "Gentlemen," she said, speaking to the angry men. "The peace treaty will return honor to America. Be assured."

"You surely heard," said one gentleman, "some six hundred runaway slaves have found sanctuary in Maryland with the British?"

I grinned to hear that, then returned my face to the mask.

"And the British took in some two thousand more slaves along the Carolinas," said someone else. "Those were our property. We have rights." The lady tapped her foot at the word *rights*. What about the slaves? I thought. Didn't they have rights?

"We are demanding that the British return our Negroes or pay for them," Miss Dolley said, smiling. "Fear not, my friends." All around the room she flowed like cool breezes, soothing tempers. After Miss Dolley passed, people smiled.

56

I tended tables heavy with vanilla ice cream, macaroons, fruit preserves, various cakes, almonds, raisins, and pecan nuts. From china bowls on graceful pedestals tumbled apples, pears, and divers berries. There were fruit punches and wine. Around the room gentlemen sipped wines and smoked sweet-smelling cigars.

My ears caught more snippets of conversation. I saw Miss Dolley take a bit of snuff from her bejeweled box. I overheard conversations about card games, chess games, gambling games, cockfighting, horse racing on a field at Thirteenth and K, North West, and theater. Two theaters presented plays from light comedy to Shakespeare's tragedies.

Everyone seemed pleased with the *National Intelligencer* newspaper. The newspaper office was at Ninth and E streets, North West, at the end of a row of handsome brick houses.

I moved smoothly behind Clementine. Half-empty food dishes we replaced quickly with full dishes. Half-burned candles were removed for full candles.

After people had finished eating, the Marine Band began to play music for a Virginia reel. Men and women chose partners, bowed, and began to dance like stiff-legged storks.

When the party was busy at dance, a slave I had never seen before took candles from me and said, "Go."

What did he mean by that? I slipped downstairs full weary from the heat. In the kitchen Aunt Sally said: "You know you have a job at chipping ice. Go, honey child."

I had never chipped ice. What did she mean?

Chapter Nine

Legs hurting and full weary, I wandered out the kitchen door into darkness among the shanties. The fresh, gardenia-fragrant outside air was cooler than the air in the Oval Room with its perfumed people, blazing candles, and smoky wall torches.

I heard crickets and cicadas making music for the summer's night. Suddenly I was sleepy. All I wanted was to tumble onto my bed mat and sleep with my soft furry kitten.

Tobias reached from behind a shed, took my hand, and led me aside. "Virginia, be you ready to help your people?"

Now? When I was so tired? But I remembered

the view from the window. "Yes, sir," I said, trembling.

"You've driven a coach. Iffen you be caught, Miss Dolley only punish you by sending you back to Montpelier. She like you."

She did? My mistress liked me? How did he know? She never smiled at me, though I tried hard to please her. I knew some grown-up slaves hated white people and made fun of them. But I was a child. I needed my mistress to praise my service. I nodded again. As I took a deep breath, I touched my treasured hair string. Maybe she did like me.

Another man drew us into dark shadows. "They think you chipping ice. Walk to the last coach on Pennsylvania Avenue and get in. Drive to Market Square and stop. If nothing happens in fifteen minutes, return and park the coach."

"But," Tobias said, "if people get in, take them where they ask, they'll tell you where, then return quickly. If a man of us do this job and get caught, he be shot. You just a child, and a merry child at that. You got a chance. Wear your bonnet."

My bonnet covered my face as I wandered past coachmen. Tobias had supplied them with wine and liquor. Many were dozing; a few argued drunkenly. No one seemed to notice me.

My knees felt like jelly, and my heart was pounding. I was on my first secret mission.

The last coach, the one I was bid to steal, had a drunken coachman sleeping in his seat. What could I do about that?

That coach faced the direction I was to go in. Could I take a coach from the other side of Pennsylvania Avenue? I crossed and peeked into that other coach. It was empty. But I feared to change my orders. I returned to the drunken coachman.

Reaching up, I pulled and pulled until he slid across the seat. I supported his head, and jerked him. He dropped to the ground and lay like a sleeping baby under the poplar tree. I felt frantic. Was that the right thing to do? Had I hurt him? Would he stay asleep?

After remembering to release the brake, I climbed into the driver's seat. My heart was drumming in my ears, and I was all a-sweat. The horses began a slow *clip-clopping* as I drove them straight to Market Square.

Where should I stop? I had to decide all by myself. Market Square was two blocks long. Five pigs wandered in the dark street. A pack of dogs I could barely see chased each other, growling and barking. Cats hissed at the dogs. I hoped dear Liberty Kitty was safe. How I yearned to curl up on my nice bed mat on the ground, hug my kitten, and sleep.

I stopped by vacant stalls midway at Market Square.

The horses snorted sleepily. When I had counted to ten, people rose out of the weeds. Strange that I hadn't seen them.

One, two, three, up to seven, then two more men slaves in tattered clothes and women in torn skirts climbed into the coach.

"Go to the foot of the bridge," said a low voice. The blue-eyed man who spoke seemed in appearance to be white. Lips that were slightly thicker and yellow hair that was wavy gave him away to me as mulatto. He was dressed well enough for the drawing room in dark suit, white shirt, and white silk stockings.

"What bridge?" I asked, in a voice that trembled.

"The first one. Will you go with them?"

Was this my chance to escape? At the thrilling possibility of liberty, I opened my eyes wide. But no, not this time. I had many secret missions ahead. I shook my head no. Besides, I would never leave without Liberty Kitty.

I flicked the reins and drove the horses slowly. A carriage passed us. Would he stop me? No. The driver seemed to pay no attention to a twelve-year-old slave girl driving.

I reached a bridge on the Potomac; I told my slaves to get out. When they left, I turned in a circle and began my return. Over my shoulder I saw two rowboats load on the men and women. A lantern flashed from a larger boat that stood off from shore.

Slowly I drove up to our block of Pennsylvania Avenue. Four turns around side streets and I drove boldly past the President's House gleaming milky white in the moonlight. I pulled the coach into its afore position. Parking beside the sleeping coachman, I even remembered to set the brakes.

Later, when I carried freshly chipped ice upstairs to the drawing room, my knees barely supported me. I had begun to tremble. But it was over now. I had carried out my first mission. I had delivered slaves to liberty.

I, Virginia of Madison, had helped slaves escape. That marvelous secret made me dizzy. I could hardly keep from singing. In truth I wanted to shout the news. Instead, I marched proudly into that Oval Room wearing my mask.

At midnight the Marine Band played "Madison's March" as our master and mistress departed the room. Then in murmuring groups the guests descended the grand staircase. John Freeman stood at the President's House door, bowing as couples and groups of friends departed.

The next morning as usual Miss Dolley was up early and ordering her household. Her other slaves and servants were used to weekly drawing rooms. Not I. I couldn't stop yawning.

Driving that coach and helping those slaves escape seemed like a summer night's dream. Had I really done that? Yes, and now I knew that Aunt Sally, Tobias, and others spent their lives aiding escapes. How I admired them!

In the kitchen they awaited drinking water for brewing tea and coffee. It was my early morning job to take the water wagon and get drinking water from a spring some blocks away. That morning I was slow delivering. Miss Dolley was listing foods for market when I returned. I rolled my water wagon beside the kitchen door.

At a glance I noticed that someone had brought Liberty Kitty in, and his cup for water sat in a corner. Beside the first sat another chipped cup. That was strange. Who would have done that? Liberty Kitty loved to roll on his back and play with the hem of my skirt as I worked, but I kept him outside. There was danger of him being stepped on in that busy kitchen.

While I stared, Rosetta Bell began to wail loudly.

"Mistress," she called, "please, blame us not for what that country child done did."

Miss Dolley looked up from her market list. "Whatever do you mean, Rosetta?"

"Oh, Mistress," said Rosetta Bell, clasping her hands and rolling her eyes, "that country child done broke two cups for her cat." She dashed to pick up the cups and show our mistress.

At that moment I recognized that the second cup was from Martha Washington's chinaware. That was precious china. Who broke that cup? Did Rosetta Bell break it or find it broken? I had not broken it, that I knew. She was making trouble for me. I moaned, and stood still as ice. There was no defending myself, and no one else would speak for me, not even Aunt Sally. Silence chilled the August heat.

Miss Dolley frowned at me. She pointed to the kitten and waved for me to remove him. Leaping forward, I scooped up Liberty Kitty and wobbled out. He seemed to know we were in trouble because he arched his back, rubbed against my chin for my comfort, and purred.

Outside I sat on an empty wine barrel and waited for my mistress's scolding. At first I was shaking so hard my teeth chattered. That Rosetta Bell told a lie on me. I would be scolded, maybe punished, and I wasn't at fault. It was a child's word against a woman's.

I waited and waited.

Miss Dolley didn't come, and I was weary to the bone. The sky grew overcast with gray clouds. When rain splattered, I took my kitten to my hut and lay down. For several hours I slept. No one called me. Rain rinsed the air to clean-smelling freshness.

When I returned to the kitchen in early afternoon, Aunt Sally ordered me to go to Market Square for butter and seasonings. Good-smelling turkeys roasted in the oven.

I looked all around, but no one else was nearby, so I asked: "Why does Rosetta Bell hate me?"

Aunt Sally glanced around. "Stay away from her."

"But why does she hate me?"

"Honey child, it ain't that she hate you, it's that she recollect a brown girl of her own that was your size."

"Where is her little girl?"

"She was a lying, lazy child, always in trouble. Supposed to do what you doing now. They sold her two years ago, honey child. Rosetta Bell been bitter-hateful ever since. Go quick to market, and hold your confidence with all. Trust no one, you hear?" I nodded, but I decided to make a plan of my own about Rosetta Bell.

In rain, Pennsylvania Avenue was a running river of mud. Walking to Market Square I overheard a coachman say: "This here city rise out of a swamp, and when it rain, this here city sink back to a swamp." So, that was it.

I removed my shoes and stockings. Squishy mud felt cool to my bare feet. My skirt and petticoats were plastered to my legs, but I bent over and kept the seasonings dry. All the way back I was thinking:

Could I make Rosetta Bell like me? Everybody said I was a brave merry child. If she knew me better, would she like me?

Chapter Ten

*O*n Sunday, August 7, we slaves were given time after breakfast to attend church in an outdoor tent nearby. The preacher read from Saint Paul's First Letter to Timothy, chapter six.

The reading told us slaves to respect our masters and mistresses, and not to do them harm. That was well and good, but I wanted to tell Saint Paul about masters, in turnabout, respecting their slaves.

I'd tell that Saint Paul about my mother and father being sold away from me; about Rosetta Bell's little girl being sold. About hunger and thirst and floggings and other suffering. I suppose my face was frowned up, because Aunt Sally bumped my elbow, and I had to put on the hide-feelings mask.

Two white men had attended services with us. When they left, we sang a hymn that turned that sermon upside down and right side up again. I sang it shouting gleefully. The words were: "God is our eternal Master, Him only must we serve!" I regained high spirits and worked an agreeable Sunday morning.

In the afternoon whilst Aunt Sally prepared dinner for four o'clock, Prisca and I stole away with a basket of juicy pink ham and yellow corn pone. Free for a few hours, we ran and walked and ran in the heat until we reached a park beside noisy Rock Creek. Prisca said the creek was swollen with racing waters due to the rain.

We passed pleasant moments eating and giggling. I wanted to tell about my secret mission, but I didn't.

Prisca did most of the talking. She stood straight, hands clasped, and said, "Oh, Mr. Madison, dearest, you are so brilliant." Then she pretended to smooth his collar as our mistress ofttimes did. I giggled and giggled.

"Oh, Mr. Henry Clay," said Prisca, "share this snuff in my pretty ruby-and-emerald snuffbox. Tell not my husband."

Then a bent-over Prisca pretended to shiver. She

pulled up her collar. "General Washington, General Washington, our fire at Valley Forge has gone out. Pray thee, what shall we do?"

She stood straight, hand across chest. "Borrow fire from the forge," she ordered, pointing at the creek. I laughed so hard I rolled on the grass.

After eating, we were loath to leave; but some strange men were staring at us. So we ran and walked and ran back to the President's House, and arrived all sweaty and dusty. My legs felt much stretched and limber.

Miss Dolley never scolded me, and Liberty Kitty kept both cups. Now when I was working in the kitchen, I locked him in a crate with open slats. In the shade outside he had water and tasty tidbits of chicken and fish to eat. My mistress ofttimes frowned at me, to keep me from being uppity, I suspect; but I kept my braids tied neatly at the nape of my neck, and I made myself highly serviceable. I prayed not to be sold as Rosetta Bell's child had been. Instead, with good work I hoped to make my mistress praise me.

All the while I tried to talk to Rosetta Bell. If only I could gain her friendship, I was sure I would solve many problems for myself. Aunt Sally and Tobias warned me to stay away from her, but I thought they were old and didn't understand her.

• • •

*O*n Monday, President James Madison was good-humored and cheerful. He and Miss Dolley were dressing to go out. Because Sukey, the personal maid, was ill of swamp fevers, Clementine attended Miss Dolley. From the window I saw her beckon to me and I remembered what Prisca had told me.

Nonetheless, I hastened upstairs to Clementine's call. In a room I passed, Master James and Miss Dolley were close in an embrace. After I passed the doorway, I stiffened in motion so as to stay still but seem to be moving. Over my shoulder I could see them in a mirror of the room.

"Today is the eighth of August," said our master, "and peace negotiations begin."

"Hold fast to hope, Mr. Madison," said Miss Dolley, playfully tweaking his ear. "England is weary of war. They will change their demands."

"And allow our expansion west? Other things are important, but we must not be bound into these fifteen United States."

"Great Britain desires no further trouble with us," said my mistress, smoothing my master's collar flap. "Now, let us finish dressing."

Strange, it seemed, that although the blue to my master's eyes was sad like the river in rain, the blue to my mistress's eyes was cheerful like the sky in springtime.

I moved quickly to the dressing chamber, and almost bumped into Clementine. In her hand she held a turban. A simple green silk turban, it had two bird of paradise feathers, and one was broken. With broken feather the turban was useless.

Clementine shoved our mistress's hat at me, and turned. If Miss Dolley had walked in at just that moment, I would have been the one holding her hat. I would have been the one blamed for the broken feather.

Hurt feelings and anger welled up within me. Clementine was involving me in trouble with my mistress, and getting out of trouble herself. She had probably broken that feather by accident, and now she was going to blame me. What should I do?

I heard Miss Dolley open an inner door. I bent quickly, pinned the turban under my skirt with the silver clip, and trod away keeping her turban hidden. The feathers tickled my legs. I heard Clementine answering questions. She said she didn't know why I was there. Having pinned that turban to my petticoat, I walked stiffer than usual. Down the stairs carefully, out the President's House I went, seeking Tobias in the horse barn.

Several servants called to me, but I pretended not to

hear. The horse barn seemed so far; heat and dampness made the air feel heavy. By the time I reached Tobias, I was drenched from sweat and fear.

Fresh hay in the barn smelled sweet. Four men were brushing horses because Miss Dolley had ordered her chariot-and-four. I turned my back, pulled up my petticoat, and unpinned the turban to show Tobias.

"Clementine gave this to me," I said, showing him the broken feather.

He said one word: "Glue."

I had hoped that he would help and he did. Using a tiny glue pot, he heated hoof glue. It seemed to take very long. When it grew soft, he began to apply it with a stick so small it looked like a splinter. I danced about in hopefulness.

One of the coachmen told me, "Sit still, why don't you?"

I tried, but I couldn't sit still. I reached up to pet a pretty bay horse on the nose. He snorted at me. The coachman showed me how to offer him a lump of brown sugar on an open palm, so as not to have my fingers bitten.

A bumblebee droned by. I moved away from it, but noticed its pretty fuzzy yellow and black. Crowds of singing flies visited the horses.

"Did you know that a black man name of Benjamin

Banneker helped survey this land for Washington City?" asked a coachman.

"Yes, sir."

"White folks ain't about to tell you that," he added, snorting like a horse. Did working around horses affect him?

I wandered over to watch. One of the men added a thin thread to help bind the glue on the feather. "It'll harden itself on the way," said Tobias, handing over my mistress's hat.

This time I held it upside down before me. That feather had to dry straight. My thoughts fluttered like a hummingbird's wings. How would I explain carrying my mistress's turban?

Chapter Eleven

How ow servants in the kitchen stared to see me carrying Miss Dolley's green silk turban with bird of paradise feathers.

As I drew near Miss Dolley's upstairs dressing room, my heart was drumming. What would I say?

In the dressing chamber Clementine stared at me as if she had never seen me before. I chose not to get her into trouble, although she hadn't given me that much courtesy. Miss Dolley was dressed in a lovely pale green dress that matched that turban. She saw me in the mirror first. Her face wore an expression of shock to see her turban in my hands.

I marched straight up to my mistress and noticed

there was a spyglass on her table. Was she using it to find her pale green turban? With great care, and a glance at the glued feather, I handed her the silk hat. What would I say? What could I say? Nothing.

I curtsied and walked quickly out.

"How did she . . . ?" I heard my mistress ask Clementine.

"Lordsy, I don't know," said Clementine, the liar. But I heard not another word because I was long gone.

President and Mrs. Madison went visiting that Monday morning. The kitchen staff was relaxed and cheerful with them gone.

*T*uesday morning I went to market with Prisca, and carried Liberty Kitty with me in my basket. I was getting him ready for our escape. In spite of bumpy walking, Liberty slept soundly in that basket.

Besides flowers to decorate the drawing room tables, we purchased butter and eggs, cherries, raspberries, dewberries, and whistleberries.

*T*he next day was the Wednesday drawing room. I was prepared this time. That night of Wednesday, August 10, I drove a coach with seventeen slaves therein. With coach springs groaning from the weight, I delivered them to the boats.

Prisca knew how to keep her confidence. That night she had scouted areas, and was a messenger. I learned about it from Tobias, but she herself said nothing. As children we were important in aiding escapes. My heart danced for joy. But, because it was a secret mission, no one could know about my brave work.

When I returned with chipped ice to the drawing room, I quickly glanced around. Eager as I was to win Rosetta Bell's approval, I had failed to gain her ear. Whenever I moved near, she ran from me. Yet she could be kind to others. One day I spied her sewing a button on French John's sleeve as he stood in the hall. Another time I saw her help the laundress hang clothes to dry. Did she think I would do her harm? I felt guilty about making her fall my first day in Washington City.

I heard her tell another servant: "That Virgie haunt me like she be the ghost of my child."

After that, I wanted even more to gain her friendship. How her heart must grieve for her little girl! As I added chipped ice to fresh punch in the drawing room, she delivered a tray of almonds. Now was my chance; I could share good news.

"Rosetta Bell," I whispered, "you can be pleased to

know that by my hand some of our brethren were freed by boat tonight." I smiled as kindly as I could, but with a roll of her eyes, she scurried away. Did she like me now? Would she admire my secret mission? Should I tell her about last January's bravery so she could be proud of me? Maybe I could be the little girl she had lost. Oh, wouldn't that be wonderful!

A week later, on Wednesday, August 17, when I drove the coach to Market Square, my blue-eyed Negro guide stopped me. "This time take them to Post Road," he whispered. "They're watching along the Potomac."

"Where is Post Road?" I asked.

He gave directions. "It travels from Washington City to Philadelphia," he said. "More danger of being caught, but we must now take the risk. Leave them by a wagon full of straw that is parked in a thicket."

Nodding, I swallowed and wet my lips. I felt so alone. I had to find Post Road all by myself. None of the terrified slaves in my coach was friendly. They were all men this time. The week before half my coach riders had been women. Some had patted my shoulder and praised my bravery, which pleased me greatly.

I drove as he directed to Post Road. It seemed a long distance from the White House. When I spied the wagon of straw, I turned my stolen coach around. Would my slaves hide in that straw? "Leave now," I told them, starting the carriage.

They dropped one by one and ran in shadows to the wagon. When they were all gone, I *clip-clopped* away at rapid speed. I felt hairs rise at the back of my neck. I didn't like being this far from the city.

Soon I heard yells. Had they been caught? I glanced over my shoulder. Should I go back for them? If I did, would I be caught? I heard shots and shouting. I drove my horses faster. No one followed me. Should I get help for them? I could trust no one on the streets. I felt wild, frantic.

I returned the coach. Where was Tobias? Where was Aunt Sally? I could tell no one in the kitchen, so I wore the mask. My chipped ice awaited me. With trembling legs I ascended the stairs. Should I share this news with Rosetta Bell? Would she listen to my fears like a mother? I needed a mother, but Rosetta avoided me! When I failed to reach her side to talk, my spirits were low.

Seeing my mistress calmed me. At that drawing room Miss Dolley wore pearls at her throat and at her wrists. They glowed against the lovely white satin of her simple low-cut gown. Her white satin turban had a gold crescent clip and a plume of ostrich feathers.

The excitement of serving at Miss Dolley's drawing

room, as always, delighted me; but what I overheard gentlemen saying made my heart flutter. One said: "Twenty-one British ships have been sighted in Chesapeake Bay."

"Do they threaten Washington City?" asked another.

"No," said his friend, "they'll attack Baltimore."

A woman asked, "Can our boys stand up to veterans of the Napoleonic Wars?"

"Oh, the British are weary of war," said her friend. "Surely they know we're negotiating peace as we speak."

Mrs. Anna Cutts, Miss Dolley's sister, told a foreign minister: "My husband is superintendent of military affairs. He says we have nothing to fear in Washington."

"No one would do harm to the city founded by General George Washington himself, and called after his name," said another lady. She laughed and daintily ate dewberries. I moved to another corner.

Was that true? Would there be fighting soon? My breath grew short as if I had climbed a hill. It seemed someplace in America would be under British attack; the soldiers on the boats may not have heard about our peace negotiations.

How I hated guns. At Montpelier I dreaded seeing deer and pheasant that hunters had killed. What would war be like? Would there be soldiers with guns? Would I see dead people?

Miss Dolley seemed to laugh and chat more than usual. "No need to worry," I heard her repeat to clusters of men and women.

I overheard a lady ask the president, "Did you hear that a fleet of British ships entered the Chesapeake?"

"We are prepared," said President Madison, with a wave of his hand. "Tomorrow General William Winder and a militia will march to aid soldiers in Maryland."

By then Miss Dolley was beside him. "No need to worry," she repeated. I thought of that spyglass on her boudoir table. Did she think to see the British land? The Chesapeake Bay led into the Potomac River, I heard. Could they sail up to attack us? The British had landed to fight a war. Why were these important people at a party when our country was in danger?

Miss Dolley smiled and chatted brightly about many things. She seemed to be trying to make everyone forget the British ships. But for how long?

In the midst of many people, I could talk to no one. I grew frantic. Would the British take me to liberty? Were they cruel soldiers, or kindly friends to slaves? The yells, the shots, the shouts. Had I delivered my slaves into a trap this night?

Chapter Twelve

The next morning was Thursday, the eighteenth of August. I had slept poorly that night. Again and again in dreams I heard the shouts, the shooting. Before dawn in the cool dark of morning I had my empty water wagon ready for my trip to the spring. But first I ran to where Tobias slept in the horse barn. Not yet had I told anyone about the night before.

"Tobias," I whispered. He answered not. A sharp smell of horse urine and manure blasted my nose and eyes. They had not cleaned out the barn.

Standing on a barrel, I peered inside where moonbeams lit the sleeping horses. Not one of the men who tended horses was there. Had they been captured in the failed escape? I worried, and began to cry.

All the way to the spring with my water wagon, I wept. I had known Tobias all my life. He served both at Montpelier and in Washington City. He had known my mother and father from the plantation fields. Only necessity for the hide-feelings mask stopped my weeping. No one must see my eyes red.

At the spring I washed my face, and held a wet handkerchief to cool my eyes while I filled the water wagon. Other slave girls gathered behind me in line. They were all atwitter, and I listened.

"The British have landed. Four thousand veteran soldiers at Benedict, Maryland."

"That be thirty-five miles northeast of the city."

"In a four-day march they could be here."

"They offering slaves a choice."

My wagon filled, I turned and suddenly they were as silent as sunrise. Had they not seen me before? I wanted to tell them that they could trust me, but I didn't know them that well.

"A choice?" I asked. By then the sky was awash with apple blossom pink. Birds murmured sleepily.

The slave girls looked at each other.

A woman said, "They telling me slaves what reach the British in Maryland can either enlist in the British navy or go to the British West Indies. Them British treat us with honor."

A girl put hands on hips. "It's runaway slaves who be leading the British troops. My uncle, he done rode back last night to tell me. And the traders, they caught twelve slaves escaping last night. They going to kill the poor wretches."

Looking at my feet, I dragged my water wagon away. My heart was pounding. Were those my slaves? Were people I drove about to be shot? What went wrong? Was I the reason they were caught?

Birdsong greeted the rosy dawn, but my spirits were too low to appreciate the melody. As I limped away, I heard someone say, "There be a spy among us for sure that done ruined that escape. I wonder if she be the one?"

"No," said someone else, "that be Virginia of Madison. She aids our African people."

So, I thought, people knew and admired me. I relished their praise, but I felt sad and lonely. At that moment I wanted to hug Liberty Kitty. I wanted to hear him purr.

As I walked, I felt deep sorrow that slaves acted as spies and would lead redcoats through the forests. Washington City was a city of promise, and America was a land of promise. But could slaves wait for that promise, or must we do what was good for ourselves now? Life in the West Indies would surely be perfect.

Every day I'll wear a flower in my hair, I thought. It was a promise I had made to myself.

Coaches and carriages passed as I dragged the White House water wagon. A coachman leaned down to whisper: "The British redcoats be marching. My son done rode back to tell me."

"The British landed four thousand strong," another man told me. "It be a four-day march to Washington City."

"General Ross got him four thousand and Admiral Sir George Cockburn, he got him twenty-two hundred seamen marching too." That man smiled.

When that coachman called to me, a colored man on the street answered his smile. "Don't you be thinking the British will do you any good. They'll abuse you like any other white men."

Was that true? Gooseflesh made my arms bumpy. Couldn't we trust them? What about all those slaves I had delivered to the British?

By the time I rolled the wagon by the kitchen door, the sky was light, and Aunt Sally grabbed my arm. "The master be wanting a pitcher of cool water, honey child. He be awake worrying all night, I'm betting."

She filled a lovely crystal pitcher and set two cut-glass goblets on a silver tray. I wanted to tell her about the shouts and shots. About delivering the slaves. But someone might overhear, and she seemed too busy.

However, carrying water to the president wasn't usually my job. I hesitated and looked at Aunt Sally. She patted my shoulder. "We who still be here got to make up for them that ain't. You understand?"

Slaves were missing from the President's House?

I set the tray down and ran outside for Liberty Kitty. Hands on hips, Aunt Sally stood in the doorway watching me.

"Keep him safe," I asked, and I put my kitten's crate in a corner of the pantry.

She hugged me to her side. "Run now, honey child."

"Is Tobias still here?"

"They got work to do. He be safe."

How heavy that water pitcher was. About halfway up the stairs I felt I wouldn't make it. Lowering the tray with shaky arms, I set the pitcher on a step and carried the goblets and tray alone. I set the tray down in the hall outside the master's bed chamber.

"No, no," I heard my master say, "those five hundred local militia are only joining our troops. American soldiers should be about seven thousand strong."

"James," said Miss Dolley softly, "is General Winder the best military man to defend our coast?"

"Yes, certainly. And we will keep one hundred guards here to defend the White House."

"Then we need have no fear," she said. "Did I hear glasses?"

When I heard her turn the doorknob, I ran for the water pitcher. As I walked back with that heavy pitcher in two hands, I saw her standing in the hall holding the silver tray. I placed the pitcher on the tray and curtsied.

"Where is Emily?" asked my mistress.

"Aunt Sally bid me bring this up."

"Where are Julia, and Etta, and Sam?"

With an impudent shrug, I curtsied and ran back to the stairs. Miss Dolley's eyes burned my back. At least she had noticed me. Smiling, I remembered the time she tied my braids back. I had washed and used that beloved string over and over.

In the kitchen Aunt Sally needed help with mixing corn pone to set in the oven. Then I sliced pink ham and arranged it like flower petals on a meat platter. It was salty, firm, and tasty. The two of us were running from spot to spot preparing breakfast, checking the oven. Then two other servants arrived.

"Did you hear the British be marching?" one asked.

"You better be marching to set them breakfast

tables," Aunt Sally said. She looked out the window, and softened her voice. "Virginia, run!"

By then I seldom hesitated when told to move. Tobias was outside behind a shed. I wanted to tell him about the failed delivery, but he seemed rushed. He took my hand, and I lumbered over to some horses.

Chapter Thirteen

I followed Tobias. At first he didn't tell me where we were going. The well-dressed, blue-eyed colored man was there. Tall and agile, he mounted a horse smoothly. Hunchback Tobias used a crate to help himself mount, then gestured for me. I rode sidesaddle behind him.

"We have to talk about your work," Tobias said. "I know they be short of help, but I thought you'd like to see this."

We cantered as master and slaves, the blue-eyed man leading. No one would doubt at a glance that he was not a wealthy young white man. Using first the river path, then empty streets, we slowly ascended a hill where others sat on horseback staring. We stopped our horses on the hillside too. There was no need for spyglass.

In the valley I saw hundreds of young men marching in loose lines. Some wore blue jackets; others, the most of them, wore ordinary clothes. All carried long guns, two different kinds. The sight of them made me ill.

"That be smoothbore muskets," Tobias said, pointing. They glinted in sunrise.

"I'd use a rifle any day before a musket," Blue-eyes said softly over his shoulder. His horse was ahead of ours.

"Most of our boys carry their own rifles," someone nearby remarked.

I was dizzy and didn't feel safe sitting sidesaddle, so I lifted my skirt and swung my leg across the horse. After all, Aunt Sally couldn't see me, and it might even help stretch my scars. The horse felt warm and sleek of fur. My heart was pounding, pounding as I watched those soldiers form in lines and march.

A man pointed. "See, there's artillery, and infantry. And cavalry on horseback. And over there the officers and staff stand reviewing them."

I suppose I should have been excited, but I viewed the soldiers with sorrow in my heart. Some might soon die; others might suffer painful burns like mine.

Tobias said: "There be the mayor."

Dr. James H. Blake, mayor of Washington City, had attended Miss Dolley's drawing room. His face was solemn.

Blue-eyes glanced behind us, and with a head toss and shrug, casually rode off. We followed at a respectful distance. When I glanced back, I saw our master and Secretary of State James Monroe. I fumbled with the bonnet hung behind me and pulled it up to cover my braids and face.

"This be Turkey Thicket," Tobias said softly. "At northeast of the city, Virginia. You might need to know that."

I felt I could tell him now. "Last night I think the slaves were caught," I said. "I heard yells and shots."

"You be smart to turn and run," he said. "Men hiding in the woods, they tried to catch our runaways. But, we be there to save them."

I was pleased that Tobias had been there to see my delivery. I squeezed his arm. He praised me for turning. Did he notice how well I handled the horses? I felt like a seagull soaring, but his next words struck me down. "But, Virginia," he said, "twelve others by the river, they been caught. Somebody done told about our Wednesday night escapes on boats. Be you knowing who?"

Blue-eyes was beside us now on his handsome black horse.

I shook my head no. A spy betrayed those twelve slaves?

"We must search," said Blue-eyes. "We have to find out who our spy can be. With the masters intent on war plans, we can empty all the slave pens from here to Alexandria. There's twenty-one British vessels in Maryland. We have a great opportunity to provide liberty to our fellow Africans."

"And I shall wear a flower in my hair," I said softly.

"What you be saying?" Tobias asked.

"Beg pardon," said I. "Just thinking of liberty."

I felt it a great privilege to view the troops assembling and marching to meet the British soldiers. When I slipped back into our White House kitchen, all were wondering whether the march had begun. I didn't say anything.

Friday and Saturday our president was in frequent meetings at the War Office. I sensed that all was not well. At one point I overheard our master say:

"Their men wear fine crimson-and-white uniforms, and march in orderly file. Only their drummers are young. Our soldiers look like boys wandering out to play."

"No need to worry," said Miss Dolley, patting his shoulder. Nevertheless, she looked anxious as well.

In the kitchen she ordered Aunt Sally: "Make extra bread."

How would bread help us? The kitchen staff was bubbling with rumors, fears, and dread, and sometimes I thought I would boil over. I could scarce stand the waiting.

Sunday the twenty-first of August Miss Dolley and her sister attended the church services of a Reverend Breckenridge. In great consternation they returned for a light afternoon repast.

Mrs. Cutts paced the room as I poured ice water. She said, "How dare the reverend lay a curse on our city!"

"He was critical of visits on the Sabbath. What better time to visit than on the Sabbath?" asked Miss Dolley, using a palm-leaf fan. "Come, Virgie, fan me."

After pouring the second glass, I curtsied and stood by her side fanning. She rested in a chair upholstered in yellow satin. Her newly arrived French-fashion dress had a shirred bodice. It was pale rose-blush pink with hat and gloves to match. How I wished I could dress in fine clothes like hers!

Wearing my hide-feelings mask, I fanned.

"Why," said Miss Dolley, "the reverend even went

so far as to say that it was sinful to have celebrations on the Sabbath."

"He called them parties," said her sister. "When Papa made us join the Philadelphia Quakers, Dolley dearest, we never had parties on Sunday." She reclined on a couch.

Miss Dolley patted perspiration from her brow. "But we are not Quakers now, Anna. And yet it concerns me greatly that Reverend Breckenridge said our city would go up in flames. He said temples and palaces would be burned to the ground." She shuddered.

After a few seconds of quiet, which passed like the ticking of a silent clock, she waved me away. "Go see about our almond cakes and pineapple, Virgie."

I curtsied and walked out with less of a limp. My scars were stretching, and my legs grew more limber by the day.

The British had been on the march from Maryland for three days. I was in low spirits and had the jitters. When would a battle begin? Although I dreaded it, at the same time I wished it were over. Maybe the time of battle would be the time of liberty for me.

Chapter Fourteen

On Monday, August 22, I returned from the spring to hear laughter in the kitchen. Prisca had a goat-skin around her shoulders and turkey feathers in her hair.

"I be Missouri Indian chief," she told me, stepping softly around the kitchen, staring solemnly at the oven and in the bread bowls.

Everyone was bent over laughing, even Aunt Sally. "Honey child," said Aunt Sally, reaching a hand to my shoulder, "you should have been here when the master have him twenty-four Missouri Indian chiefs to dinner."

Trying not to groan, I listened impatiently. Did they

not know there was a war? Besides, I was quite weary of hearing about things that had happened at the White House before I came. It seemed everything had happened before my arrival. Would anything ever happen that I could tell about?

I glanced around. We were missing about seven servants by count, but no one spoke of them. Those remaining filled in, and it was frantic work. I wondered how we would manage a drawing room, but no one else seemed worried. They talked about Indians!

"And those five white men, they be more wild than the Indians!" said another servant.

"They could talk Indian talk. White men as brown and smelly as the chiefs," said one servant.

"They smell like them leather skins. Don't take no regular baths," someone else said. "Wild men of our West. I not be going west when I leave here."

Everyone was silent when Emily said that. Everyone looked around, and I looked at Aunt Sally.

Rosetta Bell stepped in. With a glance she circled away from me and swished her long skirt. "So, where them slaves be? Escape by a boat will they? Have our slave traders beating bushes in the forest, while they sail sweet and merry-face on their way to liberty. I think I'll get me a boat ride."

Some laughed nervously. Others looked shocked.

I felt happy to have Rosetta Bell part of us. I smiled.

I still thought about her little girl and hoped she could be a friend.

Aunt Sally gave me a quick frown. Why didn't she approve of Rosetta Bell? Aunt Sally made me angry, always judging people.

French John strode in. He usually avoided the kitchen. Rather than come in, he would stand in the hall to check trays before they reached the table. Now he walked in, and excitement sparkled in his eyes.

"Zee president he is going to see zee troops," he said in breathless voice. "Make zee food for taking with."

Turning, he almost bumped the door before marching away. Now Prisca pulled feathers from her hair. "Zee president," she began, but I was already laughing.

Next came John Freeman. He spoke into our laughter, and we stopped as if a sheet of ice had chilled us.

"Our soldiers camped at Woodyard," he said softly. "But they could see the British redcoats. General Winder ordered them to fall back."

"How far did they get?" asked Aunt Sally.

"About twelve miles from here," he said. "President Madison and Dr. Thornton are going to check on the troops. They're leaving as we speak." He looked at Aunt Sally. "Do you have bread?"

They packed wheat rolls, pears, and a bottle of wine

in a basket, and John Freeman stepped smartly off to carry it. The kitchen was chilled in spite of August heat. The mercury was surely near one hundred degrees.

"If they be falling back," said Aunt Sally, "that mean they closer to Washington City. We be smelling gun smoke from that battle iffen they don't move out."

The door opened and Dan strode in. We had not seen the likes of him in three days. "I saw them," he said. His voice was hushed to a whisper tone.

"Who?" asked Rosetta Bell.

He looked away from her. Why did some people treat her that way? One of those days I would defend her.

"Our soldiers reached Woodyard," Dan said. "Then they fell back to Old Field. General Winder won't order an attack. The British . . ." He paused and moaned. He was out of breath.

"The British are all veterans of the Napoleonic Wars. You should see those red jackets. To a man they wear them. Red jackets and white pants. Gleaming muskets and bayonets. In the evening they set off rockets."

He whooshed softly and waved his arms. "Our men were eager to fight, but the red glare from those rockets . . ."

"That mean our soldiers, they be falling back

twice," said Aunt Sally. She set her bread trays on top of a cabinet to rise. In those hot days, yeast bread rose well.

Removing her apron, Aunt Sally walked out. I slipped out after her. She walked behind a shed, I followed, and she caught my arm.

"Good girl, honey child," she said. "Run now. Find Tobias. Tell him everything you done heard. Tell him I say the British be here soon. Now they cut the chains."

I nodded. Many slaves would be freed now, and I was the one carrying the news. Telling them to cut the chains was up to me, Virginia of Madison! I felt so full of happiness that my chest was about to burst.

Tobias nodded and bade me return. "Iffen the mistress say she need her coach, send Dan for me. He know where I be," he said. "Then you hitch them up. You know how."

Me? Take horses out of stalls and hitch them in proper order to the chariot-and-four? "Oh, Tobias," I said.

But he was gone. He bade me return, but I was too frightened. Would I see fighting? Would soldiers catch me? Was I in harm's way?

To hear what I could hear, I walked by the War Office, the brick building to the west of the President's House. In the doorway an officer spoke to someone I recognized from Miss Dolley's drawing room. I hid around a corner to listen.

"Robert Ross has his Fourth and Forty-fourth regiments down there. Four thousand strong. Veterans of the Napoleonic Wars. They are joined by Sir George Cockburn with two thousand sailors."

"Yes," said the other man. "It's no secret they approach from the northeast. I think General Winder hopes they'll become weary. Become exhausted and hungry from marching in this heat. He ordered our boys to fall back." He cleared his throat and added, "That puts Washington City at risk."

"All war is risk," said the officer, and walked away with not another word.

*M*iss Dolley ate alone in her room that night of August 22, 1814. President Madison did not return. Carriage after carriage passed the President's House filled with families and feather mattresses. People packed boxes and pets; they were all leaving Washington City. When my mistress did not call for her chariot-and-four, I was most relieved.

After Miss Dolley's dinner, I sat in the front yard of the President's House playing with Liberty Kitty. Were Tobias and the other men cutting chains? Who tied up the white traders? How I wished I were with Tobias.

Liberty Kitty I kept quite close. I had even put bread wrapped in a handkerchief in the basket I would carry him in. I would not go to freedom without my kitten friend, and it might be any moment now.

He had a new toy we played with, a sticky green holly leaf. Liberty carried it in his mouth to my side. He crouched and swatted it with his paw. With a stick I moved it. He leaped in the air and swatted it back.

Wherever I pushed the leaf with my stick, he would pounce on it, and swat it back to my side. When at last he grew weary of playing, he picked the leaf up in his mouth and dropped it in his basket. What a smart little kitten I had.

Smart made me think of school. No one was preparing the way for me to go. Aunt Sally had not yet asked Miss Dolley for time for me, but Prisca attended two hours a day. Would there be schools in the West Indies?

Suppose the British conquered our land? Suppose we were no longer an independent nation? What would it mean? Were the British cruel or kindly? Would we all be freed? Would freedom ever come for all Americans—Indians and Africans as well as Europeans and English?

Chapter Fifteen

On Tuesday, August 23, no slave girls were at the spring. That morning our mistress did not come down to order her household. From outside I saw her at her chamber window with spyglass in hand. President Madison still had not come home. I knew she was worried. Tobias had not returned either; others tended our horses.

That morning when there was no more work to do, Prisca and I ran to Turkey Thicket. From the hill we saw two soldiers in crimson jackets trying to creep unseen through the woods. Americans in brown and black attacked the British soldiers.

"Look," said Prisca.

"The redcoats are already here," I said, my heart aflutter with fear.

"They say they send scouts ahead of the others," said Prisca, "but those scouts got caught. Those two ain't going back to tell nobody nothing."

In two other places I spied fighting, and we heard shots. Taking Prisca's hand, I tried to pull her down the hillside. My heart was pounding and I felt faint. "We may be in harm's way," I said.

"No, we not be. See them?"

Families were on the hillside digging. Prisca and I crouched behind bushes and watched. Servants dug earth and men and women buried jewelry boxes and chinaware. One family was even trying to dig a hole big enough for a piano. Their slaves tossing dirt were sweating in the hot sunlight.

About noon, when we arrived back at the White House, Mrs. James Monroe's carriage was outside. She stood in the doorway embracing Miss Dolley. "Are you sure you won't come?" she said. "You'll be safer in Virginia."

"No need to fear," said Miss Dolley. "I'll wait for Mr. Madison. He will be here soon."

A hundred young men in blue-jacketed uniforms guarded the White House. To me they seemed like jittery farm boys dressed in uniforms and playing at soldier.

Mrs. Monroe climbed into her carriage. Her daughters, Maria and Eliza, were inside. I saw boxes, a trunk, and some food in baskets. They drove off, joining a stream of people escaping. The Madisons' houseguests had left earlier, leaving behind much of their baggage.

The mayor of Washington City, Dr. Blake, left as well. We watched his coach pass. Next door, soldiers at the War Office carted government documents away on wagons. They all headed for the bridge to travel across the Potomac River into Virginia.

*T*he next morning, Wednesday, August 24, Miss Dolley ordered a fine dinner for the evening. From her upstairs chamber she told me: "Mr. Madison will return with our victorious officers and his cabinet members. We will not have a drawing room; still, we must celebrate winning the battle."

Although it was early, she ordered me: "Virgie, tell Aunt Sally. Inform Monsieur Jean Pierre. See to it that the large dining room is set for dinner. We know not when they arrive."

Aunt Sally was not in the kitchen. When I told the other slaves, Rosetta Bell led them in laughing at me, though she should have seen that I wanted to be her friend. Why didn't she like me? What in the whole world could I offer to win her favor?

I ran to find French John. He took the news seriously. "Chere Madame Madison," he said, "zere is no battle for zee victory." He walked away shaking his head.

I wondered what he meant by that. Already I smelled gunpowder, and the night before, Prisca and I had seen the red glare of those British rockets. It had been exciting and scary at the same time.

A sad-faced Aunt Sally stepped wearily through the kitchen door. I told her: "Miss Dolley wants a big victory dinner for the president, his officers, and his cabinet members."

She glanced around. "Why ain't you moving in here?" she said, hands on slim hips.

Now, thin Aunt Sally was straight at the hips. Even in petticoats and skirts, she had no hips. Behind her Prisca formed the soundless words: Why ain't you moving in here? and she kept putting fists on hips. But her hands slid down. Again and again her fists would not set on her hips.

I ran out the door so Aunt Sally wouldn't see me laughing. It seemed strange that the British were there, and we were joking. Others were coughing and choking from laughter as they turned to work. While I was out, I ran to the barn.

Tobias opened the door. He pulled me inside and set the latch. The barn held some hundred or more slaves. Men, women, and children were quietly eating bread and drinking water.

I clasped my hands and smiled. More liberty for our slaves. I felt pleased that these trader slaves were no longer hungry and thirsty.

"You know Analostan Island?" Tobias said. "Well, others are waiting there, but the British on the Potomac ain't taking slaves yet. There be a battle at Bladensburg."

"Bladensburg? That's close."

"About five miles from the Capitol. General Winder had our soldiers fall back to the village of Bladensburg. Our soldiers are in three lines facing the redcoats in the northeast."

One of our other coachmen said, "They tell me the British hesitated to attack men out of uniform. We have seven thousand to face their four thousand veterans and two thousand sailors, and this is our land. We'll see an early victory."

"I ain't counting on that. General Winder done broke our men's spirits," Tobias told him. "When he kept ordering them to fall back, they be confused. Marching in this heat. And they ain't been fed. Unless they carried their own food, they ain't had a bite to eat. They ain't ready to fight."

I returned to the house. Since we had no flowers purchased for the dinner table, I decided to gather "garlands of greenery" from Tiber Creek's edge. I planned to set holly and bay leaves in bowls of water on the table to please my mistress.

But by the river, Liberty and I had to hide. I could hear cannons and smell gunpowder. Two men with rifles stumbled past. I gathered some greenery, oak leaves this time, until I saw a British soldier sitting and staring at the water. His bright red jacket lay by his side. His pants were white.

I set Liberty Kitty on my apron in the basket and ran toward the White House. Now that my scars were more stretched, my legs felt strong in running. Hearing footsteps, I crouched in bushes. Five men in blue jackets stumbled past me. They looked neither right nor left. One dropped his musket in passing.

A slave of Washington City ran out and picked up the musket. He sniffed it, and said: "That soldier be running and he ain't never even shot off his gun."

He picked up five other guns from the bushes and strolled away. What did it mean for slaves to gather guns? Would there be an uprising?

Now, running to the President's House, I circled to the front. Mr. Carroll, one of the Washington City commissioners, was at the door talking to Miss Dolley.

"You must flee the city. My coach is at your service,

Mrs. Madison. The redcoats will be here this evening or sooner."

"Thank you, Mr. Carroll. We have coaches aplenty, but our guards have all fled. One hundred guards Mr. Madison left me, and all have deserted." She wrung her hands, and peered up and down the avenue.

Just then two men galloped up on horses covered with sweat and frothing at the mouth. "Mrs. Madison," called one. "The president bids you flee. He tried to cross the bridge and found himself riding into General Ross's army. He is well, but he bids you flee Washington City."

From where I stood, I saw her smile. I suppose any news from the master was welcome, even bad news. "I am grateful for the news," she called.

The riders galloped away.

"And I'm grateful to you, Mr. Carroll," she said. "We are packing now."

In the kitchen all servants and slaves wore sad faces. "Our spirits are low, honey child," said Aunt Sally when I walked in. She paced the kitchen floor clasping her hands.

"What happened?" I asked.

"They ran," said about five people at once.

"I don't know what we be boiling veal and ham for," said Rosetta Bell. "And chilling wine in the wine cellar. Only folks who done had a victory be them British."

"They won?" I asked, astonished. Was the war over?

"The British done walked over them," Dan said, glancing out the door. "Our soldiers be spread out in three lines facing the British to fight. General Winder, he order the first line to fall back. They had to run through the second and third lines. Soon they all be a-running."

Another slave looked in the door. "Ain't no Battle of Bladensburg," he said. "They calling it the Bladensburg Races."

He beckoned to me. Since I didn't recognize him, I looked to Aunt Sally. She nodded. Outside he grasped my arm tightly. "Tobias need you."

Chapter Sixteen

This stranger would have dragged me away then, but first I ran for Liberty Kitty. Sleeping in his crate, he stretched as I settled him in the basket next to my bread. I ran out.

At the horse barn Tobias was waiting. "I be needing you to drive a carriage north to Philadelphia," he said. Post Road led straight east, and then north to Pennsylvania.

I was pleased that I had thought to bring Liberty Kitty. Philadelphia meant freedom for me as well as for the other slaves. The Madisons had two fine carriages, and no one on the Post Road in this heat and excitement would ever stop me. But suppose Miss Dolley needed her chariot? How would they explain its absence?

Inside the chariot I saw baskets of food and buckets of water. The closed chariot hid raggedy women and bare-chested men.

I was all set to drive the horses out of the barn when Dan knocked on the door. "Our mistress, she done sent for her coaches," said he. "French John and John Freeman be packing her up."

Tobias raised his arms in the air. "Now how do we get them free? Looking like trader slaves, they ain't about to escape in open carriages or on wagons. Wouldn't get nowhere."

Dan and others opened the coaches; I climbed down with Liberty Kitty. Part of me was sorry, part of me glad. An idea tickled my mind, but I kept silent. I ran back to the White House. In the front foyer all was frantic activity. Slaves carried crates out to the coaches now driven around to the front.

"See to it that you take care with that," Miss Dolley called, waving a handkerchief. "That box contains a precious copy of the Declaration of Independence. And in those boxes are Mr. Madison's cabinet papers."

"Where is zee White House guard?" Monsieur Jean Pierre asked, staring out the front door.

Miss Dolley began to cry. "They have all abandoned me. Thank God some of my slaves are loyal."

Wiping her eyes, Miss Dolley straightened her shoulders. "God fits the burden to the back," she said.

As I carried her bag downstairs, I had to admire her. All my life I had sought her approval. I had tried hard to please her, but I now realized that I wanted to be like her too. My mistress was a woman of courage.

At the bottom of the steps, Sukey snatched the bag from me. She looked thin and wan from her attack of swamp fever. "I be the one to carry her personal things. I be her personal maid, not you!" Sukey need not have been jealous of me.

All that was packed in that bag were papers important to government. Miss Dolley carried practically none of her own things. No feathered turbans or gowns or even jewelry did I notice among the boxes. Her personal bag held only a change of clothes and a gown for sleeping.

That idea yet tickled my mind. What would we do about our slaves in the horse barn ready to escape, and dependent on us?

French John began removing the fine portrait of General George Washington from the wall. I liked that picture of President Washington. It had been one of the earliest things to catch my eye as I entered the White House that first day. French John and John Freeman were having difficulty as I followed my mistress back upstairs to her bedchamber. Miss Dolley had asked me, and not Sukey. Dizzy from excitement, I heard my heart pounding in my ears. It was almost two o'clock in the afternoon.

In her bedroom Miss Dolley stood with spyglass staring out the window. Without spyglass I could see American soldiers running, walking, stumbling. Our army was running away. When would the British army arrive? I held silence, but wrung my hands. My mistress must hasten or she might get caught.

She pulled out her stationery and began to write. I heard her whispered letter to her sister in these words:

Will you believe it, we have had a battle near Bladensburg. And, I am still here within sound of the cannon. Mr. Madison comes not. May God protect him. Two messengers covered with dust come bid me fly, but I wait for him.

When I walked back downstairs behind Miss Dolley, they were still struggling to remove General Washington's portrait. Heart pounding from excitement, I sat on the stairs.

French John said, "Zee frame, it is screwed into zee wall."

"Well," said John Freeman, "ain't nothing left but to cut out the canvas."

"John, you're wise," said Miss Dolley. "Roll the

canvas. These two gentlemen from New York will take it to safekeeping."

The men from New York had been at our drawing room, but could we trust them?

Soon both chariot and coach were leaving. Along with boxes of important papers, Miss Dolley and Sukey rode in the chariot-and-four; John Freeman and French John rode with crates and boxes in the second carriage. I waved good-bye until I could see them no longer.

Jewelry, chinaware, silverware, objects of gold, sculptures, finest fashions from Paris, all were abandoned.

After they drove off, Aunt Sally came to sit beside me on the front portico steps. Liberty Kitty and I played our leaf game. Liberty pounced on the holly leaf and tossed it high. Whenever I dragged it back with a stick, the kitten swatted it away. Now I felt calm.

"Them British be here tonight for sure," said Aunt Sally. "French John, he done locked up before he left."

"But I can climb in any window," I said.

"You sure can, honey child."

"We must eat, and others as well." By others I meant our slaves. All that food was prepared for a victory dinner celebration. Should it go to waste?

"Iffen somebody open up, I be doing my work in

114

the kitchen. But I don't want to see who done opened up the White House."

I caught Liberty Kitty and shoved him into her arms. Running around back, I tied my long skirt up, jumped, and caught a sill. Then I climbed in a window. As I dropped inside the dining room, I realized my leg scars were mostly stretched now. I strutted without a limp to open the kitchen door.

Dan, Aunt Sally, and I went out to the slaves in the horse barn. Tobias was gone because Miss Dolley had insisted that he drive her chariot-and-four. We led the slaves to the White House, and bade them wait outside.

Prisca ran in. "The redcoats be here," she called. "From Turkey Thicket I done seen them marching." She bent over to catch her breath.

I said, "Suppose they steal Miss Dolley's clothes and jewelry? What a shame that would be, when we could use those clothes."

Dan, Aunt Sally, and Prisca stared at me.

"Why should they be wasted when our African brethren want for covering in their escape? And money for their spending?"

"You mean," said Aunt Sally slowly, "we loyal slaves give away the jewels and clothing of the President's House?"

"Yes," I said. I had thought of clothes of only the

master and mistress, but the guests had been all sizes—fat and thin—and even had children. Their clothes had been abandoned as well.

Hands raised, Rosetta Bell swished around the doorway where she had been hiding. "I heard you," she called, pointing. "I be telling Master what you thinking of doing."

"Just like you done told on our slave escapes by boat?" asked Dan.

Tossing her head, Rosetta Bell said, "I ain't no spy, but I got that story free. For that information I be paid enough to buy my freedom. If I wanted, I could be at liberty soon. But you all gonna be shot!" She laughed and ran out.

So shocked was I that I could hardly move. *I was a traitor.* How angry they would be to know that I had spoiled the Wednesday night escapes. My prattle let Rosetta Bell know the means of escape. She got the story free from me! My mouth hung open.

For money she betrayed us, betrayed her own people. Aunt Sally and Dan had been right about Rosetta Bell after all, but I had been too muleheaded to listen.

I had wanted her to be a friend, and she had betrayed me. She never knew how much I cared about her. Yet, pressing my lips together, I held my confidence. That was now past. I felt sure I would take this guilt to my grave. Why had I so needed people to like me, that I became a traitor? A traitor by prattle!

"What we be waiting for?" asked Aunt Sally, breaking into my misery. "Iffen we be shot for stealing White House clothes and jewelry, let's us give them good enough reason."

There was work to do. I jumped up. "Dan," I called, "Tobias told me more slaves are hiding on Analostan Island."

"I be going for them as we speak." He ran out.

Chapter Seventeen

Over the grand White House staircase railing I threw clothing: pantaloons, shirts, jackets, gowns, turbans, men's shoes, women's shoes, children's shoes, children's pantalets, children's dresses. Clothes fluttered through the air like pear blossom petals in springtime.

Out the window I watched Prisca boldly take all the trader slaves down to Tiber Creek. They seemed delighted to splash in the cool waters. After all had bathed, she led them to the White House.

We ate veal, ham, chicken, cabbage, sweet potatoes, corn bread, wheat rolls, almonds, pecan nuts, small cakes with preserved pears, apples, berries. A victory celebration there was after all. It was now about six o'clock in the evening.

Dan helped the men dress. He even gave quick haircuts. Aunt Sally chose clothes to fit the women. Prisca and I handed out children's clothing. Our white masters and guests had need of many clothes; each slave desired but one outfit to ride proudly into liberty.

I asked their names and former masters. The slaves turned and pranced and smiled at their new clothes. Some hugged themselves and laughed aloud. "What will happen when they reach Philadelphia?" I asked as I buttoned up a boy's shirt.

"When *you* reach Philadelphia," said Dan, correcting me. "Virginia, we be needing you to drive along with the others."

Aunt Sally said, "In Philadelphia there be societies from colored churches and Quaker people. They treat our brethren like Christian people ought to. They find them places to live, jobs to work, schools for grownups and children to attend. You be liking Philadelphia, honey child."

"Do they have flowers in Philadelphia?"

"Why, honey child, they sure do. Why you be asking?"

I shrugged. "Will some still go with the British?" Since the British had beat our soldiers in battle, I felt strange about them. After all, they were the enemy.

"We be clearing out slave pens everywhere we can reach, and others be doing the same," Dan said. "There's boats taking some down the Potomac to British ships in Maryland."

I decided that Liberty Kitty and I preferred Philadelphia. I could be loyal to my African people and stay in America. However, haunting my mind were the words: Virginia is a traitor by prattle!

Oh, what sorrow I felt. In trying to gain Rosetta Bell's friendship, I had caused twelve slaves to die. I grieved for those people. Were there children among the men and women? As they died, did they wonder who had revealed their escape? Twelve slaves shot because of my prattle.

A well-dressed slave rode up to the back of the White House. "The first redcoats arrived about four o'clock," he said. "Their officers are here on horseback now, but there's trouble brewing."

"What trouble?" asked Dan. We had dressed over two hundred slaves and still clothes were available.

"Someone has fired a rifle at the British from Mr. Sewell's house on the northwest corner of Second Street and Maryland Avenue. A British soldier was wounded, and that made the British angry. Now the redcoats have set fire to Mr. Sewell's house. And General Ross has marched his men to the navy yard to do more mischief."

"Where's the navy yard?" I asked.

"It be by deep water at the Anacostia River," said Dan. From all over the city he had found abandoned wagons and horses. Now we led everyone out front to Pennsylvania Avenue.

I smelled gunpowder and saw rockets' red lights on the horizon. But the strangest sight was Miss Dolley's gowns on beautiful colored women! We had a front yard of the best-dressed Africans in America. Those slaves would escape in grand fashion, fashion from Paris. It looked like a gracious drawing room of brown-skin people.

At sunset, the sky was lavender and lovely. In spite of sorrow, my heart leaped joyfully. Strange, that joy and sorrow could be so close.

We handed out pieces of jewelry. "Sell this for money," said Aunt Sally, walking from one to another.

I even took the crescent pins from Miss Dolley's turbans. Those I kept in my basket with Liberty Kitty. I might need them.

I drove two horses pulling a wagon with about thirty people crowded on. We sat four across on the driver's seat. I felt so excited glancing back as one wagon after another set off for the Post Road, and this time I knew the way.

At a turn a man called to us: "The redcoats are burning down the navy yard." I nodded to him.

We joined other wagons on Post Road. A white man who passed us called: "General Ross has ordered his men to burn down our Capitol. The dome is in flames. Look behind you at the next hill." He seemed not to notice that we were escaping with slaves.

"I'm grateful you told me, sir," I called.

At a curve a well-dressed black man who had been walking along turned and stood in the trees. "Missy, be you driving north?"

"Yes, sir," I said. "Going to Philadelphia."

"I be walking there," he said. "Could I beg a ride?"

At that moment we were atop a rise. Looking back I saw Capitol Hill in flames. The sky was dark, and the flame's brightness reflected off clouds in the sky. Washington City was burning. My heart began to drum in my chest. I took a deep breath.

Our Capitol Building was burning. Tobias had promised to let me climb Capitol Hill. I had wanted to roll eggs at Easter on Capitol Hill. Where was I going? Was I a Virginian, or a Pennsylvanian?

The man held the reins to my horses. I could offer him a ride, but four of us sat crowded across the driver's seat, and every inch of space was taken in the back. Strange that he should stop me.

Washington City is burning, I thought, and a sob caught in my throat. I snatched Liberty Kitty and the basket, took out my loaf and jewelry, and kept my white handkerchief.

"Here's bread, and jewels for selling," I told the man. "Follow the road. If a man named Dan asks about me, tell him I've returned."

I gave the man my seat. Taking the reins expertly, he started the horses. My slaves called, "Good-bye, Virginia. Good-bye!"

I waved to them. Barely had I crossed the road, when a rider galloped toward me. Using my white handkerchief, I waved him to stop.

"What do you want?" asked the man, using the pause to consult his pocket watch.

"Sir, President James Madison is my master." My heart was pounding, and tears wet my face. "I must return to Washington City."

He swung me up behind him. I held his coattails with one hand, Liberty Kitty's basket with the other. He galloped on.

"What time is it, sir?" I asked.

"It's ten thirty," he said. "Is there trouble in the District of Columbia?"

"Washington City is burning," I said.

And half an hour later, when he set me down in front of the President's House, I saw a most extraordinary sight.

Chapter Eighteen

The pungent smell of burning wood and smoldering plaster penetrated the night air. Flames from other fires lit the sight before me. At first I felt terrified as I watched, then I grew angry.

Soldiers in red jackets and white pants ran out the front door of the President's House and stood around the portico comparing souvenirs. Others drank bottles of fine French wines from our White House wine cellar. I wanted to jerk those bottles out of their hands.

"To King George the Third!" they called. Bottles and fine crystal wine glasses were raised in a toast, hundreds strong. They dared toast their king with our president's wine?

I backed across Pennsylvania Avenue and stood against a poplar tree. Strange emotions struggled within me. Part of me wanted to run away; part of me wanted to strike out at those British soldiers in their fine red and white.

Although a slave child, I had never felt more American. I was born in America. My mother and father, and their mothers and fathers were born here. I wasn't free, but this was a land of freedom's promise. Our Constitution said so.

Was mine a role in history?

Soon an admiral swaggered out the door. "Order the fire brigade," he called.

Soldiers ran out the White House. A group of fifty men—seamen and marines—surrounded the President's House in orderly fashion. They lit balls the size of dinner plates. The burning balls were swinging from the ends of long poles.

At a command, they crashed the balls of flame through the windows of the White House. At first there was flickering light from each window. Through the doorway I saw chairs piled in the foyer for burning. Soon the first and second floors were blazing. Grief dwelt heavy in my heart. I had loved our gleaming White House. Liberty Kitty watched from my shoulder.

A voice at my side said, "Now they'll never miss

them clothes, Virginia." I managed to smile at Aunt Sally, and squeeze her hand. "We mostly working back at our old master's house. Find somewhere to hide till the Madisons come back, honey child." When I looked again, she had disappeared.

Next, they set fire to the War Office and Treasury Building on either side of the White House. The heat across the street grew intense. With a crowd I followed the British soldiers and sailors, my basket over an arm, my kitten on my shoulder. We Americans tramped in sad-face silence.

One man said, "Whereas they had veterans, we had young mechanics and farmers in our army. Many of our boys never carried a musket before."

"We are a brave people," said a woman. "It was not so much fear as prudence that caused our retreat."

A redcoat officer of high rank walked up.

"General Ross," a woman called, "please do me the favor of sparing my home. We have six children who live there."

So this was the famous general. I felt small honor in seeing him. In spite of his fancy uniform, I hated him because he ordered death and destruction.

The general bowed to the woman. "I will order it spared as you ask, madam. If Mrs. Dolley Madison had been home, I would have spared her palace. We will burn the homes only where people have run from us."

Spirits low, I followed the crowd.

At Ninth and E streets, North West—the office of the newspaper—the British admiral stood with British seamen and called: "Here we will set a fire. After burning Jemmy's palace, my friend Josey would be affronted with me if I did not pay him the same compliment." He waved.

By Jemmy I supposed he spoke of my master, President James Madison. And by Josey, I supposed he meant Mr. Joseph Gales, co-owner and editor of the newspaper.

Women standing outside had homes ajoining the *National Intelligencer* office. Mrs. Brush and Mrs. Stelle were among them. "If you so please, Admiral Cockburn," one called, "burn not this office. Our homes are on this row. All the houses will burn with the newspaper office."

The admiral said, "Then I'll not burn it. See, I'm not a savage and ferocious creature as Josey represented me. I'm quite harmless, ladies. I'll take better care of you than Jemmy did."

I had heard that the newspaper criticized the admiral. How did he find out? What did he expect the newspaper to say?

"So, lads," called the admiral, "take your axes, tear down the office, and burn the newspapers in the street. I have no argument with ladies."

Some of the ladies called out: "We are most grateful, admiral."

"But," called Admiral Cockburn with an arm raised, "find the newspaper press within. Rub out the letter *C* so my friend Josey can vilify me no longer."

As his seamen took their axes to the building, the admiral showed off his souvenirs. "See what I took from Jemmy's palace," he called. Among them I recognized a pair of dueling pistols given my master.

Over my shoulder I heard a man say, "At the navy yard they burned our two new ships under construction, and the frigate that was finished."

"Cinders have set the wooden homes near Capitol Hill on fire," said a woman.

Weary and confused, I wandered along until I reached Market Square. I ate pears and berries scattered on the ground in a fruit stall. I gave water to Liberty Kitty from a horse trough, and we slept on trampled grass, hidden in a stall.

Each time I raised my head in the night, I saw yellow fires. My betrayal by prattle ate at me like a worm in cabbage. My spirits were low. My kitten friend and I were alone. Aunt Sally and Prisca were serving their masters.

• • •

Next morning was Thursday the twenty-fifth of August. I fed Liberty Kitty some bread crusts in sour milk I found in back of a house. I feared to make myself ill if I ate the same.

Guilt and grief played tag racing through my mind. Shame tiptoed between them. I had betrayed my people. Drawn to Tiber Creek, I knelt and began to pick up stones. I chose twelve round black stones and held them in my hands and heart at the same time. Because of my silly prattle, twelve people had died.

By creek's edge, I found a mossy glen. There I knelt and placed my twelve black stones in a circle. "Liberty Kitty," I whispered, "guard them."

While my kitten sniffed ferns, I wandered seeking wildflowers in pink and yellow and purple and white. These flowers I placed within the circle of stones. It was a cheerful sight. I then prayed for those twelve slaves, and asked for strength to be steadfast in service for liberty from that day forth.

When I picked up Liberty Kitty, I walked away with new resolve. And a small measure of peace.

Remembering that all those wagons of well-dressed slaves were now closer to freedom raised my spirits. No one had praised my plan to dress escaping slaves for their journey. Why should I wait for someone to praise me? I decided to praise myself.

"Good work, Virginia," I said aloud. "You're a smart and clever girl." I patted my face with Liberty's paw.

Joining a crowd I wandered to the Patent Office at Eighth and E streets, North West, on the northeast corner. Admiral Cockburn and his marines were there, and Dr. William Thornton stood speaking to him. Since President Madison had left with this same Dr. Thornton to view the troops, I greeted the sight of the doctor with cheer.

"Sir," said Dr. Thornton, "you can't burn this building. As a museum of arts, its loss would be a tragedy to all the world." The handsome Patent Office Building was also the office of our government's postal service, and the post office of Washington City.

"Why then," said the admiral, "I will order that this fine building be spared. I am no villain." He rode an old white mare with long mane and tail. Behind me some women whispered that his manners were more like a common sailor than a dignified commander.

One lady behind me whispered to another, "Dr. James Ewell is a traitor. He offered his home at First and A streets, North West, to the British admiral and general. They slept there last night."

Weary of soldiers, I returned to view the blackened ruins of our President's House. A few stones of the walls stood; however, part of the roof had crashed down into the cellar. Small flames here and there flickered. The bulk of the White House smoldered sadly. In back all the wooden sheds, stalls, and slave huts had burned.

My pretty White House dresses and shoes were gone. All I had in the world were the clothes on my back, and the kitten in my arms. I could no longer cry. I think my tears had dried up like a shallow river in dry weather. Except for Liberty Kitty I was alone in Washington City. What now?

Chapter Nineteen

At noon on Thursday, sipping spring water, I sat in grass on the lot across from the White House. Liberty Kitty purred on my lap as I rubbed his silken tiger fur. Guilt and loneliness dampened my spirits, but I remembered that God is good, and is forgiving of our faults. Therein was my comfort. I refused to wallow in self-pity. I must go on.

Citizens of Washington, Maryland, and Virginia rode past on horseback staring at the ruins of the President's House. A brisk breeze stirred the ashes, and by that Thursday evening the sky blackened with thunderclouds.

Gusts of air blew cinders and ashes everywhere. I pulled my bonnet forward to cover head and face. As the wind grew stronger, it wailed through the ruins of our White House, and soon rain pelted Pennsylvania Avenue.

Leaning into wind and sheets of warm rain I crept to my Market Square stall, but it was flattened. By now my shoes and skirts were slippery from mud. I saw a rider blown off his horse. The only good thing about the rain was that it put out the lingering fires.

The ditch I tried to crouch in soon filled with water. Liberty Kitty was frightened by crashing thunder and lightning that scorched a blackened sky. I saw British soldiers and sailors by the thousands, huddled together in the downpour. The wind grew like unto a hurricane.

I clung to an oak trunk and crouched over my kitten's basket to keep him somewhat dry. All the servants and slaves I knew had masters to return to. Alone in the city, I thought about Aunt Sally, Tobias, Dan, and the others. I mused on this month in Washington City and what it had meant in my life. Did Tobias flee to freedom after driving Miss Dolley?

The British admiral and some sailors rode up to a pump where an American lady pumped water. "Great

God, madam," said the admiral. "Is this the kind of storm to which you are accustomed in this infernal country?"

"No, sir," she said, "this is a special interposition of Providence to drive our enemies from our city."

I smiled in the rain. The redcoats had burned our city, but they had not destroyed our spirit!

"Not so, madam," the admiral told her. "It is rather to aid them in the destruction of your city." And he and his redcoats rode off with the last word.

In spite of British soldiers in the city, I was not afraid. I saw no cruelty to ordinary people. Many were in hiding, I supposed, but I had nowhere to hide. When the wind died down briefly, I wandered in warm rain to find out what was happening.

By Dr. Ewell's house at First and A streets, I watched the British officers hold a meeting in the streets. The crowd of uniforms parted from time to time as men carried wounded soldiers inside.

"Will we leave our wounded at the mercy of these Americans?" I heard an officer ask.

"Dr. Ewell seems a respectable doctor and gentleman," said another. "He has promised to care for them."

Many Washington City people with angry-looking faces passed that house in the rain. "Traitor!" they called to the doctor.

Soon after their meeting, the officers moved among the soldiers. Slowly they began walking toward Bladensburg. They appeared to creep away in the dark of wind and rain.

On the street a woman asked me, "Have the British left?"

"Yes, ma'am," said I. "Leastwise some of them."

I stood with rain running down my face.

That night I found a grassy space beside a beech tree. A barn wall had collapsed against the tree, and it formed a snug shelter. The weather continued warm; Liberty Kitty and I were as comfortable as sadness would allow.

By Friday, August 26, all the British who could walk were gone, and only the wounded remained. As I wandered the streets that morning, I came upon bodies among the weeds. Both redcoats and blue had died in skirmishes.

Around noon I found a cloth bundle with rolls and fruit and ham. It was next to a dead American soldier. I took the food back to the barn wall. Liberty Kitty and I sat sheltered from warm drizzle and hungrily ate the feast; and I saved some for later. There was less wind, and the rain was now light.

•   •   •

By noon Saturday, August 27, the rain had stopped. I walked to swollen Tiber Creek behind what used to be the President's House. In privacy there I bathed and washed mud from my clothes. When my clean clothes were somewhat dry, I dressed. The boom of cannons firing spoiled the quiet.

"Virginia," Prisca called, as she burst through the bushes. I turned to see Prisca and Aunt Sally.

"Where'd you stay, honey child?" But before I could answer, Aunt Sally went on. "I was with my master who hires me out to the White House. His wife was low in spirits, and I took care of his children." She pointed. "I hear them cannons is from Fort Warburton."

"Look," Prisca called. She pulled Miss Dolley's spyglass from her skirt pocket, and pointed. "The British are at Alexandria." By spyglass I saw their ships, sailing frigates of war.

We made a shelter of sorts by Tiber Creek. Prisca and I found food in the White House cellar, some bread and ham that had survived the fire. That night we ate and slept together.

The next morning, Sunday, August 28, Tobias woke us up. He had brought our mistress back to the city. "Have all the British gone?" he asked. But he knew the answer.

I hugged him; I was surprised at how pleased I was to see him. "Are you well? Where have you been?" But I knew the answer.

"You children," he said to me and to Prisca, "it not be too late to go with the British to the West Indies. We have boats of slaves leaving for Alexandria in an hour."

Aunt Sally hugged Prisca to one side and me to the other. "You children be young. Have a whole life ahead of you. It be different for me." How loving her hug seemed.

Yes, I thought: You, Tobias, Dan, and the others live right under the nose of the president, and help others escape. That takes a special dedication.

I had admired my master and mistress, but what about the slaves I knew? Had I given them the respect they deserved?

As we spoke, we strolled around to Pennsylvania Avenue. A parade of people were returning in coaches and wagons. Another cannon boomed. A white man with twitching face came up to us. "Do you slaves have any rifles or muskets?" he asked in a low trembling voice.

"No, sir," said Aunt Sally.

A slave behind the man was toting a crate full of collected ammunition and guns. The slave smiled at me, and I smiled back. I felt an understanding; there was no need for an uprising.

When the man walked on, Tobias turned to me. "Well?"

I picked up Liberty Kitty. Purring, he arched his head to rub beneath my chin. His purring was a loud, lovely song. Now was my moment, mine and Liberty's.

Chapter Twenty

A few hours later I stood outside Mrs. Anna Cutts's home at 1333–1335 F Street, North West. That Sunday morning when Miss Dolley had returned, her sister had invited her to stay there.

On the street outside the house Miss Dolley saw the Reverend Breckenridge, and called to him: "I little thought, sir, when I heard that threatening sermon of yours, that its denunciation would so soon be realized."

"Oh, madam," he said, "I trust this chastening of the Lord may not be in vain."

Later she spoke to us as we stood in the kitchen. "I wept," she said, "how I wept to see the President's

House destroyed. It had been built for generations to come. Now, only blackened walls remain." Her tears flowed, so that she left the room overcome with grief.

We waited in a long line of servants, among them Tobias, Aunt Sally, Dan, Rosetta Bell, Liberty Kitty in arms, and me.

Dan asked Rosetta Bell, "You have your traitor money. Why didn't you escape to freedom?"

"Who, me?" she asked. "Dig dirt on some scrabble farm? Dress in rags and half starve in the name of freedom?" She laughed. I looked away from her.

I had looked for a friend in Rosetta Bell, who despised me. Now that I had given up that frantic search for love, approval, praise—I found myself surrounded with it. I stood between Tobias and Aunt Sally.

During that month of August, I had been spoiled with favors. Yet I had taken for granted Tobias, Aunt Sally, Dan—people who truly cared about me. People who gave me treats, who trusted me, who loved me. I saw praise reflected in the warmth of their smiles. That grieving hole in my heart was healing now with the biblical balm of Gilead—*love*.

Miss Dolley walked back to us and dabbed her reddened eyes.

"We have been in Virginia, Mr. Madison and I," Miss Dolley said, struggling to speak. "But here in

Washington City what the British destroyed not, the hurricane spared not."

With lacy handkerchief, she waved at us. "Now you will be ordered by my sister's servants for their aid. There are not slave accommodations enough for you. You must sleep outdoors somewhere. We will be here, Mr. Madison and I, until we can secure a proper home in the city."

"Mrs. Madison," Rosetta Bell asked, "be there money for loyal slaves to tell on traitors? You should know what happened when you be gone." She grinned and rolled her eyes.

Somehow, I was not afraid. Since I was now a slave by choice, I decided that I owned myself. I had disobeyed no master. As that hymn had said, "God is my eternal Master, Him only must I serve."

Prisca had left on the freedom boat to join the British in Alexandria. However, I felt at liberty as well. I had made a choice for the next two years: to aid those who wanted to escape. If I had gone to freedom, there would have been one free slave girl. If I stayed like Tobias and Aunt Sally, there might be hundreds of slaves that I could help.

Only two more years remained in my master's term as president. After that I might go to freedom, or I might return to Montpelier. For now I would be in Washington City.

In Washington City I could attend school for a colored child. Serving leaders of a new nation gave me a place in history, and I dressed and ate well as a White House slave. Having both family in Aunt Sally and Tobias, and a future in aiding liberty, I truly possessed a wonderful role for a child.

But if we were turned over as traitors by Rosetta Bell, there would be no future for any of us. She stood grinning.

"Rosetta Bell," said Miss Dolley with a deep sigh, "you must understand something. When I was a mere girl of twelve or thirteen, my father freed his slaves in Virginia. We moved to Pennsylvania. He made us into Philadelphia Quakers who struggle for liberty for slaves like yourselves. Slavery is not to my liking."

I frowned. How could I have admired a mistress who bought, allowed abuse of, and sold slaves against her beliefs? Never before had I seen her in this light. She had betrayed her Quaker childhood. How could I have wanted to be like her?

Miss Dolley sighed again and said, "However, Mr. Madison and I are Virginians, and we uphold Virginia's laws. That is all I will say to you."

As she turned to leave her sister's kitchen, she stood, back turned. A bowl of fresh pink roses sat on the small kitchen table before her. "Thank you," she said, in a low trembling voice. "I thank those of you who are here for being loyal slaves."

She plucked a rose and turned to me. "Virgie," she said, "I think it proper for you to wear a flower in your hair." Miss Dolley pushed the stem of the fragrant pink rose into one of my braids. She knew not what it meant.

But I knew. Although there would be difficulties, I would joyfully accept waters from a peaceful spring at dawn. And I knew that I, Virginia of Madison, had remained right where I wanted to arrive.

Author's Note

In the 1790s Washington City was planned to excel in beauty the capitals of the ancient Greek and Roman empires. Black astronomer Benjamin Banneker assisted in surveying the land. Only a day's buggy ride from George Washington's estate at Mount Vernon, the site is on the Potomac and Anacostia rivers.

However, by 1814 this dream city was the principal East Coast slave market. There were auction blocks for selling slaves on the Mall; and parades of shackled slaves walked South Capitol Street and Pennsylvania Avenue in front of the White House.

Among 10,000 residents in Washington in 1814, there were 1,800 slaves and another 1,700 free African-

Americans. Theirs was an elite society. Three slaves, George Bell, Moses Liverpool, and Nicholas Franklin, opened a school for African-American children in 1807. There was also a school in George Town on Dumbarton Street run by a Mrs. Mary Billings. Many of these African-Americans were proud to be part of the early days in Washington City.

Diaries of early Washington white people showed fear of a slave uprising, and gratitude that the slaves were meek, loyal servants. Nonetheless, those meek slaves escaped both by wagons and boats. Slaves of influential people, even Daniel Webster's servant, helped in freeing "trader" slaves. So many slaves ran away to the British during the War of 1812 that one of the demands for the peace treaty was for return of the slaves.

The unpopular War of 1812 was declared for freedom on the high seas. Americans also wanted to expand to our western and Canadian frontiers without British-Indian interference.

After the burning of Washington City during that war, many were angry. A wall showed this graffito: GEORGE WASHINGTON FOUNDED THIS CITY AFTER A SEVEN YEARS' WAR. JAMES MADISON LOST IT AFTER A TWO YEARS' WAR.

The British never returned to Washington, but in September 1814, Georgetown lawyer Francis Scott

Key saw a battle against the British at North Point in Baltimore, Maryland. He wrote a poem about it called "The Star-Spangled Banner."

In the 1800s communications took weeks by land or months by sea. Two days before President James Madison asked his Congress to declare war, the British repealed the laws of impressment that were the reasons for the war. And our successful Battle of New Orleans against the British was fought fifteen days after the Peace of Christmas Eve had ended the war.

Some have called the War of 1812 the second war of independence. After the war no slaves were returned, no Indian barrier states were set up, and there was no limit to our expansion. Furthermore, the states were more united; had developed industry in independence from England; and had begun to expand westward.

This story is historical fiction. Virginia, Tobias, Aunt Sally, Rosetta Bell, Dan, and others are fictional characters. As far as I know, there were no trader slaves held or clothed at the White House; and Miss Dolley's dresses burned in the White House fire. While slaves of influential people in Washington helped free trader slaves, I have no research to prove that White House slaves worked with them. On the other hand, I have no proof that they did not assist in escapes, either.

In researching the history behind this story I have

used diaries and material from accounts before historical societies. For each day of this story, all wartime and most White House happenings are true. I have attempted to keep real people true to their personalities, and much of the dialogue during the burning is verbatim from historical reports. Besides the well-known American and British historical people, the Reverend Breckenridge of the famous sermon, the butler-doorman John Freeman, Mrs. Madison's personal maid Sukey, and master of ceremony Monsieur Jean Pierre Sioussant are also real.

Into the White House of August 1814 marched Virginia of Madison. May this story of slavery and injustice of yesteryear challenge us to work for freedom and justice today.

Bibliography

Froncek, Thomas, ed. *An Illustrated History of the City of Washington.* By Junior League of Washington. New York: Alfred A. Knopf, 1977.

Furman, Bess. *White House Profile.* New York: Bobbs-Merrill Co., 1951.

Hickey, Donald R. *The War of 1812: A Forgotten Conflict.* Chicago: University of Illinois Press, 1989.

Klapthor, Margaret Brown. *Official White House China, 1789 to the Present.* Washington: Smithsonian Institution Press, 1975.

Lloyd, Alan. *The Scorching of Washington: The War of 1812.* Washington: Robert B. Luce, 1974.

Madison, Doll(e)y. *Memoirs and Letters.* New York: Houghton Mifflin, 1886.

Smith, Margaret Bayard. *The First Forty Years of Washington Society.* Charles Scribner's Sons, 1906. Reprint. New York: Frederick Ungar Publishing Co., 1965.

Thornton, Mrs. William. *Diary of Mrs. W.T.: Capture of Washington by the British.* Columbia Historical Society, Washington, D.C., vol. 19. Washington: Columbia Historical Society, 1916.

Weller, M. I. *Dr. James Ewell's Report. Unwelcome Visitors to Early Washington, August 24, 1814.* Columbia Historical Society, Washington, D.C., vol. 1. Washington: Columbia Historical Society, 1897.